## 'Is it too soon to kiss you?'

'No. . .' Willingly and with heat rising in her like warm bread, Thea turned into Joe's arms and tilted her face. His lips quested unhurriedly, exploring the taste and feel of her. It was a long time before he pulled reluctantly away, to look at her in the moonlight. She looked at him as well. But each saw much more than small physical details. They saw a potential future. . .

**Dear Reader**

This month we complete Margaret O'Neill's quartet with TAKE A DEEP BREATH, based around the accident and emergency department. We go to Australia with Lilian Darcy in NO MORE SECRETS, where the need to conceal Thea's romance with Joe leads to problems, and introduce a new Australian author in Meredith Webber, whose HEALING LOVE takes us to a burns unit in India — Leith and Gabe are fascinating people. We round up with TILL SUMMER ENDS by Hazel Fisher — warm thoughts as we move into spring!

*The Editor*

**Lilian Darcy** is Australian, but on her marriage made her home in America. She writes for theatre, film and television, as well as romantic fiction, and she likes winter sports, music, travel and the study of languages. Hospital volunteer work and friends in the medical profession provide the research background for her novels; she enjoys being able to create realistic modern stories, believable characters, and a romance that will stand the test of time.

**Recent titles by the same author:**

HEART CALL
A PRIVATE ARRANGEMENT

# NO MORE SECRETS

BY
LILIAN DARCY

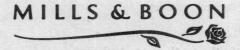

## MILLS & BOON

MILLS & BOON LIMITED
ETON HOUSE, 18–24 PARADISE ROAD
RICHMOND, SURREY, TW9 1SR

First published in Great Britain 1994
by Mills & Boon Limited

© Lilian Darcy 1994

Australian copyright 1994
Philippine copyright 1994
This edition 1994

ISBN 0 263 78476 2

Set in 10 on 11 pt Linotron Times
03-9403-56701

Typeset in Great Britain by Centracet, Cambridge
Made and printed in Great Britain

# CHAPTER ONE

'ARE you wearing *that*, dear?' Pamela Carmichael fussed around her daughter like a timid bumble-bee, her voice high and hesitant.

'Yes,' said Thea, a little shortly. 'And I thought you liked it.'

'Well, I do, but. . .' Mrs Carmichael stood back and studied the neat cream sundress, her bird-like head cocked to one side.

'What did *you* want me to wear?' Thea questioned, trying to mask her irritation.

'I thought. . .your suit.'

'My *suit*?'

It was ridiculous! All this fuss over a simple lunch with Grandfather Carmichael. As for the suit, Thea had bought it several years ago to wear for nursing interviews, and its tailored navy and white skirt, jacket and blouse would be hot and uncomfortable on this baking January day in Sydney. How typical of her mother, too, to turn a casual lunch with Grandpa into a formal and terrifying occasion!

It has always been this way. Would English-born Mrs Carmichael never realise that it didn't *matter*, here in Australia, that a grocer's daughter had married into an old and rather distinguished medical family? Actually, it probably didn't matter in England any more either!

Thea studied herself in the mirror for a moment, trying to screen out the nervous, fretful face that still hovered behind her left shoulder. The sundress was neat, new and attractive. Her shoulder-length hair, too pretty a shade to be called 'mouse-brown', was clean, freshly brushed and held in place with fashionable clips. A few simple strokes of make-up here and there added freshness and colour to sparkling grey-green eyes and well-tended, lightly tanned skin, and she wore a delicate gold necklace around her open throat to add some more sparkle. In short, she looked just right for lunch in the city with a grandparent and she wasn't going to let her mother spoil the occasion by transmitting a contagious case of nerves.

'I'm *not* going to change now, Mother,' she said firmly. 'If I do, I'll be late.'

'Oh, goodness, that would never do. Go, then, right away, in case the train is early. . . And for heaven's sake, don't tell your grandfather about David's motorbike.'

'I won't, Mother,' Thea said on a controlled sigh as she allowed herself to be propelled down the passage and out of the front door so quickly that she would probably be waiting for the train for at least fifteen minutes.

It was a relief to be walking down the jacaranda-shaded footpath towards the station. The Carmichael household had been such a cloying place in the twelve years since her father's death. She wasn't surprised that eighteen-year-old David had bought a motorbike on which he now roared away from the house at every possible opportunity. No doubt his restlessness was prompted by the same irritation that had led Thea to move into a flat with a fellow nurse last year.

'It's so convenient to the hospital,' Thea had told her mother. 'And Charmaine and I are such good friends.'

This last part wasn't strictly true. Charmaine Tandy was twenty-six to Thea's twenty-three, rather brash and on occasion very sophisticated. Thea wasn't sophisticated at all, especially when it came to men. . .which seemed to be Charmaine's main area of expertise. Boys had been interested in Thea since her mid-teens — boys, and now, gradually, men — but Pamela Carmichael had frightened them off, or frightened Thea, with her nervously expressed questions about their background and intentions, so that the young nurse was unusually inexperienced for her age, and wistfully hoping that that would soon change.

For this reason she sometimes enjoyed Charmaine's worldly company, but their friendship was more a matter of convenience, and what with busy nursing shifts and busy personal lives they didn't spend too much time together. But at least it satisfied Mrs Carmichael.

With some more of her mother's warnings echoing in her mind, Thea got on the train and was carried away towards town. 'Don't tell Grandpa I sold the Pepco shares.' 'Don't ask about Cousin Andrew. Grandpa will think I've been gossiping.' 'Don't tell him about David's summer job. I know no one in the Carmichael family has ever been a petrol-pump attendant before!'

With all these secrets to keep track of, Thea found that the contagious case of nerves had been through its incubation period and was now breaking out into full-blown symptoms. Her stomach began to flutter and her throat tightened. Grandfather Carmichael had been a distinguished professor in the medical faculty at Sydney University before his retirement. Thea was only a humble nurse. He'd probably be bored stiff if she started prattling about her job, and he surely wouldn't be interested in her friends and social life. . .

Oh, heavens, what on earth *will* we talk about? she wondered.

\* \* \*

'Well, this is very pleasant, isn't it, Thea?' Dr James Carmichael said as he sat back in his chair, pushed away the empty plate that had held quiche and salad, and picked up his freshly poured cup of tea.

He was still a distinguished-looking man, with a full head of iron-grey hair and intelligent blue eyes. The Australian sun had taken its toll on him, though, as the skin of his face and hands was lined and marked with several rough dark spots.

'Mmm, yes, it is,' Thea answered him sincerely.

She couldn't remember now why she had been nervous an hour ago. Grandpa always had such interesting things to say, and he never gave the slightest indication that he was trying to sniff out those subjects which Thea's mother was so determined should not be discussed. So far, in fact, they hadn't talked about anything personal at all. Grandpa had told her, instead, about his work for the National Parks Association, and, very wittily, about his role in dealing with a recent problem in the organisation.

'I'm sorry Hester couldn't come up,' he said now, referring to Thea's grandmother. 'She's very busy with preparing for our trip.'

'That's right!' Thea exclaimed, remembering. 'You're off to England and Europe in five weeks, aren't you?'

'In four weeks and six days,' Grandpa Carmichael said, trying to sound blasé and world-weary about it, but acknowledging by the twinkle in his eyes that he had failed dismally.

'You can't wait, can you?' Thea teased.

'No, but it has created a lot of work. We're house-swapping with some friends in England for part of the time, so Hester decided we needed to repaint our place and clean out every nook and cranny. By the time it's all done we'll be too tired to actually go!'

Thea laughed. What a splendid pair they both were, and yet she was only just beginning to realise it. Why did Mother have to spoil things so often with her silly fears and secrets? For years it had put up a barrier between the senior Carmichaels and their son's children — a barrier that was only just beginning to break down. For a moment Thea had a wild urge to tell Grandpa every detail she could think of about David's motorbike, his summer job, the Pepco shares, Cousin Andrew's divorce, and any other unsuitable subjects that came to mind, but she managed to resist. She said instead, with an excitement that matched her grandfather's, 'I'm going away myself in a few days.'

'Aha! So you've caught the Carmichael travel bug!'

'I think so. I've never really been away before, so perhaps I'll hate it.'

'You'll love it. What's it to be? Tasmania? The Barrier Reef?'

'New Zealand. Just the South Island. Three weeks of camping and hiking with an organised wilderness tour for young people.'

He frowned, and for an awful moment she thought she had committed one of the conversational gaffes her mother was so afraid of. 'It's not fair, you know, Dorothea!' he exclaimed energetically. 'Why are these marvellous wilderness trips only for young people? Do you think if your grandmother and I dyed our hair we could pass for thirty-four?'

'You probably could,' Thea laughed, forgiving him for frightening her with that frown, and for using the full version of her name, which she thoroughly disliked.

'Dorothea' had been another of her mother's ideas. It was a Carmichael family name, belonging to an ancient and rather well-to-do aunt of Grandpa's, but, if Pamela Carmichael had been hoping that Great-Aunt Dottie would leave her money to her young namesake, she had been disappointed. Miss Dorothea Carmichael, on her death ten years ago, had left a very clear will that directed all her assets to cancer research.

'Three weeks,' Grandpa was saying now. 'That's a nice juicy chunk away from the hospital.'

'Yes, it is.' She sensed that he was probing a little. 'It'll be good to get away. No matter how much someone loves nursing, the atmosphere of a big hospital can be stressful at times.'

'You do love it, then?'

'Oh, yes! I'm a very small frog and the hospital is a very large pond—*too* large, I sometimes think,' she admitted. 'But every day there's some particular satisfaction that makes what I do seem important and fulfilling. Sometimes, I——' She stopped, realising that a retired doctor of his stature must have heard or felt all this before.

'Go on, Thea,' he prompted.

Quickly editing, she said, 'Nothing, really. I'm just glad that I chose the Carmichael family profession, that's all.'

He only nodded, his slightly faded blue eyes narrowing thoughtfully for a moment, but Thea could see that he was very pleased at what she had said. They sipped their tea in silence for a few minutes. Thea realised that the small city restaurant was getting quieter as people returned to work or to shopping. Time had passed quickly.

Now Grandpa was speaking again. 'I'm glad you do think of it as a family profession,' he said slowly and thoughtfully. 'Your father would have made a brilliant medical researcher had he lived. Ex-colleagues of his and mine ask me whether David is going to follow in his footsteps. Any idea what I should tell them?'

Thea thought of her mother and suppressed a sigh. She could hear Pamela Carmichael's voice, 'Don't tell

Grandpa about. . .' in her mind, and at first it held sway. Thoughts ticking rapidly, she tried to find something tactful, non-committal, pleasing to hear. Then she rebelled. No! Why fob Grandpa off as if he were too sensitive or too ogre-like to be told the truth?

'I don't think so, I'm afraid.' She spoke with careful honesty, staring down at the neat fingers that were fiddling with her napkin. 'He's not planning to go to university at all at this stage.' She looked up. Grandpa was nodding cautiously. Taking another steadying breath, she went on, 'He wants to start his own business eventually, so he's planning to do some courses in accounting and business management.'

'What sort of business?'

'Video movie rentals or electronic games.' There! It was out!

'Ouch!' said Grandpa cheerfully. 'Rather him than me. . .'

'I know you must be angry. . .' Thea blurted.

'Angry?'

'Yes. I mean. . .'

'No, not angry,' Dr Carmichael mused. 'Disappointed? Of course, yes, a little. Surprised? Again, no. From what I've seen of David——' Thea could hear in his tone a suggestion that he had not been allowed to see enough of his grandchildren '——I'd say games and videos were more his line. He'll probably do well out of it. I'm glad he's realised it now rather than at the end of several punishing years of medicine.'

'Yes,' said Thea, inexpressibly relieved. 'That's what I tell Mother——'

'Ah! So you've discussed it with your mother?'

'A little. Not a lot.' Thea had lost her courage again. Grandpa didn't need to hear about his daughter-in-law's tears and exaggerations, her entreaties to David, her transparent attempts at emotional blackmail. Thea had already done enough damage. Pamela Carmichael hadn't even thought to say this morning, Don't tell Grandpa about David's career plans, because the secrecy of this particular family drama was so well understood by each of them that it wouldn't have occurred to Mrs Carmichael that Thea might let the thing out.

But Grandpa had reacted in his usual marvellous way. Why does Mother misunderstand him so dreadfully? Thea wondered in a moment of love and pity. Then she squared her shoulders and spoke aloud. 'So it's up to me to carry the torch, and I'm only a nurse, not a doctor.'

'*Never* say only a nurse,' Grandpa came in firmly. 'Your grandmother was a nurse before we married, and if I hadn't already had the utmost respect for the profession she would soon have drummed it into me!'

'I'm glad you think so,' Thea laughed. 'Too many doctors still don't!'

'But as for carrying the torch of medicine. . . Since it *is* by way of being a family profession, you mustn't ever hesitate to come to me if you have a problem or a question—or an ambition! For example, I have a good friend who is very active in the Royal Flying Doctor Service. Not that I'd pull strings for you in any way that was unfair to other people, but information, a job interview. . .'

'I'll remember that,' Thea said sincerely. 'Thank you. I can't think of anything at the moment, but if I ever do I'd be proud to have your help.'

They smiled at each other, and Thea knew that she had made her grandfather happy. Swallowing the last mouthful of her tea, she decided that it was a good feeling.

\*    \*    \*

'Day One. Meet with your fellow tour members for an informal get-together in the hotel's reception area at six p.m.,' Thea read from her tour itinerary. It was four o'clock now, her watch told her. That was two o'clock Sydney time — although travel books always warned you not to keep track of your home time-zone.

Stretching with luxurious anticipation on the bed, she considered her options. Food? A nap? Lunch on the plane had been a novelty for a young nurse unused to flying and she had eaten it all, so she wasn't hungry. The day seemed long due to the dislocation of travel but she didn't feel tired. Instead, the hotel swimming-pool beckoned. Since they would be 'roughing it' for the rest of the tour. . .

Five minutes later she was beside the sparkling water, dropping her towel carelessly on a lounging-chair before testing the water with a neat, pointed foot. Gorgeous! Confidently, she plunged in head first, rose to the surface in a fluid motion, rolled on to her back and lay there, floating and kicking lazily. Utterly gorgeous!

Concerns about her mother's and David's difficult relationship, thoughts about her favourite patients on the general medical ward at Sydney's Mount Royal Hospital, the over-sweet, artificial scent of the aero-plane. . .all these washed-away as she lolled in the water. She felt very happy about her new bathing-suit, too. The colourful turquoise background of the classic one-piece was enlivened still further by a pattern of splashy gold leopard spots, to create a bright, holiday look that reflected her happy, carefree mood.

Someone else was looking at the new turquoise and gold bathing suit, too, and at the pretty young woman who wore it.

I wonder if she's coming on the tour? Dr Joe Stockwell thought to himself. I hope so. . .

He had wanted to say hello to her when she entered the fenced and landscaped pool area but she hadn't even seen him, had just gone straight to the inviting water. He liked the way she had dived in so gracefully and confidently. Too many women shrieked and fussed as they tiptoed down the steps at the shallow end, and he couldn't stand that. Some people never risked getting their bathing suits wet at all, just came to the pool or the beach to work on their tans, and if there were any of that type on this rugged camping tour they could make life miserable indeed!

This was Joe Stockwell's third day at the hotel here in Christchurch, and his sixth swim in this refreshing pool. He had wanted to come over a few days early, knowing he needed a good chance to unwind before the tour started. This past year of residency at South Sydney General Hospital had been long and hard, and he suspected that if he had jumped straight into a demanding schedule of hiking with a group of strangers he would have struck all of them as a grumpy, funless specimen.

Now, after two and half days of exploring Christchurch in a leisurely way, he felt a lot better. He had been at the pool for an hour before the arrival of the young woman in the turquoise suit, churning up and down the length of it a hundred and twenty times, which he had calculated was getting on for a mile. Now he lay on his towel in the sun, his muscles loose and relaxed as only a good work-out could make them.

He was allowing himself to tan and freckle a little today, though normally he was a fairly strong believer in sunblock cream. The statistics on skin cancer in Australia were sobering. . . But for once the hot bake of the sun on his bare, muscular back was very pleasant.

Studying the newcomer once more from under the

careful screen of long dark brown lashes, Joe wondered, Should I go up to her? Introduce myself? Ask her about the tour?

He decided against it. There was something very private about her pleasure in the water. Splashing and humming now, she looked as if she was letting a similar weariness and similar anxieties to his own wash away, and he hated the idea of interrupting or trespassing. In fact. . . Joe turned his head away and closed his eyes again, feeling that it was a violation of her privacy even to be looking at her. . .

As it happened, however, his concerns about privacy were shared by Thea herself. She had only just noticed the prone male figure lying on a towel in a sunny patch of grass near the low stone wall on the far side of the pool. Had he been there all along? He must have been. How dreadful! She had blithely intruded on his solitude, splashing about — and *humming*! — without so much as the courtesy of a murmured hello.

She wondered whether she ought to go up to him now, but he was lying so still that she thought he might have dropped into a doze, in which case a disruptive greeting would be ruder than leaving him alone. Was he a fellow tour member? she wondered, trailing her fingers absently through the chest-deep water. With that thick hair lying sleek and still wet against his head and that firm, muscular back, he certainly looked young and fit enough to be a camper and hiker.

I could ask, she realised, but again she was reluctant about the idea. The tour group would get acquainted soon enough. Turning on to her back, she did several lazy lengths of backstroke and then, since the prone figure was *still* prone and motionless, she got out of the pool, dried herself quickly and tiptoed quietly out of the pool enclosure.

\* \* \*

It was definitely her, Joe Stockwell decided. Silky light-brown hair was fluffed around her face now instead of falling, darker and straighter, on to her shoulders as it dripped with water. That slim yet deliciously curved figure was different, too, disguised by baggy beige shorts and a light blue denim shirt, but still it was definitely the girl from the pool.

She stood a little uncertainly on the edge of the loosely gathered group, clearly wishing she had something to do with her hands, or a place to sit, or someone to talk to. There were about a dozen people gathered now. A few of them were grouped around the tour leader, who looked — Joe considered — absurdly young to be leading a wilderness trip. Most of the others looked as if they knew each other already, or had drummed up the beginnings of an acquaintance earlier in the day.

Joe looked at the tour leader again. Can't he see that she's feeling left out? he thought in irritation, and without waiting any longer he crossed over to the young woman, forgetting to feel any of the diffidence one normally felt at approaching a stranger.

Thea saw him coming towards her and her heart thumped. He was going to say something jolly. He had noticed she was feeling shy. He felt sorry for her! For a moment, she hated the whole situation and almost turned aside, intending to shoulder her way into the clutch of people gathered around the tour leader, who had introduced himself as Cliff.

She realised in time, though, that it was too late. The stranger was almost upon her, his tall figure towering above her so that she had to look up quite a distance to meet cheerful, intelligent blue eyes. He smiled at her and she pressed her own lips into a reluctant curve, anticipating some inane line. He was very good-looking, she realised, and the fact didn't

please her. Thick brown hair with reddish glints, high
cheekbones, a very straight, firm nose and just enough
freckles to give him a charmingly boyish look. . . He
was probably the type to think she'd be flattered at his
attention.

But when he spoke. . . 'That was you I saw at the
pool this afternoon, wasn't it?'

'Yes. At least. . .was it you lying on the grass? I
thought you were asleep.'

'I almost was, after you'd gone.'

Then they both spoke together. 'I didn't want to
disturb you.'

He threw back his head and gave a rich chuckle
while Thea was thinking confusedly, What a lovely
voice he has! So nice and low and sincere. Not the
brash, over-confident tone she had been expecting at
all.

'I like the way you dived into the pool,' he was
saying now.

'Oh!' she exclaimed, flustered. 'I'm not much of a
diver.

'I didn't mean your score for technical merit,' he
smiled. He had nice lips, smooth ones, not too thin or
too full, and they curved slowly into a smile as if even
his sense of humour was a thoughtful one. 'I mean the
way you tested the water just once, then let yourself
go.'

'Oh, that!' She considered the comment for a
moment, and found that she understood what he
wanted to say. 'You mean I don't shilly-shally?'

'And you don't squeal.'

'I do squeal sometimes,' she admitted, screwing up
her neat nose. 'In the ocean, the first swim of the
summer when it's still cold.'

'That's acceptable,' he conceded. 'The Pacific Ocean
can be pretty chilly.'

'Let's gather, shall we?' Cliff called out now. 'Everyone's here, if I've checked my list right. Now, some of you don't know everybody yet. But is there anyone who doesn't know anyone else at all?'

'I don't know anyone,' Joe said quietly.

'I don't know anyone either,' echoed Thea, feeling shyness and apprehension return.

But then her eyes met Joe's, and suddenly she knew that it wasn't true any more. They knew each other.

# CHAPTER TWO

THEA stirred a large pan of yellow egg, scraping it away from the pan's bottom as it began to set. Beside her Cathy, who shared her tent, turned pieces of crisping bacon with barbecue tongs. It was half-past six in the morning. Normally Thea's stomach and taste-buds were very definitely not open for business at that hour, but here in the wild open air she had quickly shaken off the stiffness that came from a night on a thin foam mattress pad and was already ravenous.

The air was so fresh here! Looking up from her cooking, she could see her fellow campers at work on dismantling their tents or returning from an early-morning scrub in the camping-ground's simple bath-room. At a wooden picnic table Barry, another member of her cooking team, was buttering toast he had made on a wire grill over the fire, and beside him, making tea and setting out big enamel mugs, was Joe.

Thea felt a heat rising in her that had nothing to do with the fire in front of her. This was the twelfth of January, the fourth day of the wilderness trip, and the powerful sense she had had that first night that she and Joe Stockwell already knew each other had not diminished. Indeed, it had grown. In this sort of situation you found out about people surprisingly fast.

'Looks just about ready.' It was Joe himself, his tall, capable figure suddenly telescoping as he squatted beside her to warm his hands by the flames.

'It is,' she agreed, giving the fluffy mixture a last few turns then taking the pan from the fire.

'Mmm! Smells fabulous. What did you put in it?'

19

'I found a jar of mixed herbs in the supply box and added a pinch or two, as well as black pepper.'

'This bacon is as crisp as I can make it without burning the lot,' came in curly-haired Cathy cheerfully. 'Why don't you ring the gong, Joe?'

'I'm planning to do just that,' he returned, stretching himself into a standing position once more. As he did so, his hand brushed briefly against Thea's shoulder, a touch that might have been accidental. . .or might have been a caress.

Last night the two of them had stayed for what felt like hours in front of this fire, having a late-night hot chocolate and talking lazily about. . .everything, it seemed. Everyone else had gone to bed long before, and Thea knew it was only Joe's awareness of today's long hike that had made him say with undisguised reluctance when the camping ground was utterly silent, 'We have to get to bed — or we won't make those fifteen kilometres tomorrow.'

She had agreed and they had parted company at the dying fire, since their tents were pitched on opposite sides of the rough circle around it and the picnic table. Walking to her tent, she had been unable to resist one look back at him and, turning, she had found that he had stopped and turned to look at her as well. He had raised a hand then disappeared into the darkness as he bent towards his tent flap.

Now, pouring coffee, she remembered the gesture. It had seemed to promise so much, and she knew already that she wanted all of it.

'Today's our first really tough day, as you know,' Cliff said as they ate.

Jancy, a rather plump, giggling girl who had come — reluctantly, Thea suspected — with her boyfriend Peter, groaned and slumped down in her seat. Cliff frowned at her absently and went on, 'We'll drive straight to the trail-head this morning, gear up and set off. We won't see the tour van again till we reach the far end of the track in four days, so we'll be carrying all our food. The track is over fifty kilometres altogether, and some of it is rough. If anyone thinks they won't make it, better say so now and we can arrange for you to stay with the van.'

He frowned again, a forbidding expression as it betrayed very clearly that he hoped no one would be such a nuisance as to want to stay with the van.

'How is the van getting to the far end of the track, if you're coming on the hike with us?' Jancy asked.

'The tour company has a back-up crew that does that sort of stuff,' Cliff explained, running a hand through coarse black hair. 'They have a few vans to move for the different tour groups, so they have some schedule of their own, apparently, and they'll meet us at the far end with fresh food supplies.'

'So you don't know whether they'll come for the van today or tomorrow or what?' Again it was Jancy.

'Er —' Cliff flicked quickly through some pages fastened to a clipboard, gave up and said simply, 'No, I don't, I'm sorry.' There was a short silence, then he spoke again. 'So. . . I take it everyone's up for the hike?'

A murmured chorus of assent came from the group, but Thea noticed that Jancy didn't actually say anything. She suspected that the plump girl was not too confident about her own fitness and would have opted out of the four-day hike if the alternative had been more attractive. A possible two- or three-day wait for the back-up crew? No, thanks! Thea was glad she had spent the past two months in training for this trip, even though at the time carrying a backpack loaded with rocks and a sleeping-bag around the suburbs of Sydney had seemd a rather silly way to spend her spare time!

Finishing her breakfast quickly, she went to help Cathy dismantle their tent so that the two tour members who had volunteered to be the loading team could start packing the gear on to the van's substantial roof-rack. Soon everything was ready, Cliff climbed into the driver's seat and they were off.

'You said the terrain of the track was pretty rough?' Peter asked as they drove.

'Yes, in parts,' Cliff answered.

'What's it like scenically, then?'

'Oh, it's great!'

Suddenly the tour leader was animated, sketching out a vivid picture of the history, geography, geology and wildlife of the region. This was clearly his area of expertise, and he was good with most of the practical things as well — helping the cooking team to light their fire, explaining the map, parcelling out a fair load of provisions for each hiker to carry in their packs. With people, though, he wasn't as adept.

I wonder how long he's been leading these tours? Thea wondered.

An hour later they were on the track, and once again Thea was glad she had practised with a backpack. The path led up and down over rocks, gravel, boggy patches, and hard, smooth earth. At first there were distant vistas of the glinting Tasman Sea to the west, then, as the sun rose in the sky and the day warmed, ridges were crossed that cut off this backward view and instead the dominant sight was the mountains, many of them still white with snow and the ice of glaciers.

Jackets and pullovers soon came off, and at the first resting place, where packs were thankfully swung to the ground, most people exchanged long trousers for comfortable baggy shorts.

Thea, in blue denim, sat on a rock chewing on a handful of nuts, chocolate pieces and dried fruit, feeling very content. The hike was a challenge, no doubt about that, but it was wonderfully satisfying as well. Beneath the thick trees it was cool and damp, and the sense of isolation from the outside world was splendidly refreshing to the spirit. She watched Joe stretch out his lightly tanned throat as he gulped down cold water, letting it splash carelessly over his chin and chest because it felt so cool that way, then she reached out her hand as he gave her a brimming mug and did the same as he had just done.

'Doesn't water taste *good* sometimes?' he said to her — a simple comment, quite ordinary, but said in a quiet tone that meant it was just for her.

Later, they had an hour's break for lunch, boiling a billy-can on a tiny fire for tea and munching on the huge corned beef and salad sandwiches they had cut that morning before leaving the camping ground. When she had finished her sandwich, Thea took her tea and wandered off by herself, wanting to find complete solitude for a while. The forest was alive with sound, but it was such a different quality of sound from what she knew in the city that it almost felt like silence.

Then she heard a more human noise and Joe Stockwell stepped quietly out of the undergrowth. He smiled at her and she went up to him, seeing the camera slung around his neck. 'Did you get some good shots?'

'I hope so.'

'Oh, did you see something unusual? An animal or a bird?'

'Unusual?' he smiled crookedly. '*I* thought so. I just photographed colours and textures. Tiny things, mostly. There are some really beautiful mushrooms back beyond that fallen log, and other fungi as well. You probably think ——'

She anticipated his words. 'No, I don't think you're

weird to be photographing fungi. I've seen some beautiful colours and shapes today. A brilliant orange, and some perfect fluted things clinging to an old tree-trunk, all striped in colours that looked like different layers of chocolate.'

'Chocolate? I bet they don't taste that way!'

'I wasn't prepared to find out,' she grimaced.

'And I hope no one else is feeling experimental. I doubt our combined medical skills are equal to dealing with a case of mushroom poisoning out here in the wilds.'

They laughed, then she said reluctantly, 'Hadn't we better get back?'

'I think so.' He seemed equally loath to rejoin the group.

They had found out on that first evening of introductions that they were both medical people, and the fact had at once deepened the instinctive bond that had sprung up between them. Now every talk they had and every moment they shared seemed to be doing the same thing.

I wonder if I'll ever think about toadstools and mushrooms in the same way again? Thea thought as she walked beside him back to the lunch spot, her insides flowing with a warm, giddy and extremely pleasant feeling.

After lunch, the track seemed to grow harder. Perhaps it was tiredness creeping over everyone, perhaps it was the boggy terrain they traversed — along a steep slope that fell away on one side to a magnificent roaring river — or perhaps it was a bevy of maddening sand-flies that hovered around the group, seeming to keep pace with them like a crowd of bloodthirsty autograph hunters.

Insect repellent was slathered on and hot sun or gusts of breeze that temporarily thinned the insects'

numbers were greeted with universal relief. Even the
sand-flies, though, couldn't spoil Thea's pleasure in the
hike. They passed two groups of 'trampers' — as New
Zealanders called them — hiking in the opposite direction, and were told each time, 'It gets even better. You
should see the waterfalls! And the view of Mount
Aspiring.'

Thea didn't need to be told that it got better. She
would enjoy the view of Mount Aspiring when she got
to it. Meanwhile, glimpses of unique New Zealand bird
life such as *keas* and *tuis*, and the constant sound of
rushing water in her ears, was enough.

Jancy, though, was heard to mutter, 'Mount
Aspiring? It should be called Mount Aspirin! I've got
such a headache.'

Thea saw Joe look expectantly at Cliff, who had also
been within earshot. Several others were further ahead
almost out of sight. Cliff had stopped for a few minutes
to point out to Thea, Joe and Cathy a pair of paradise
ducks and to talk with his usual enthusiasm about the
different species of beech tree that formed the forest
canopy. While he was still talking, Jancy had reached
the group, red-cheeked, hot and irritable, with Peter
trying to jolly her along.

Cliff didn't say anything in response to Jancy's
indirect request for a headache tablet and at first Thea
thought he hadn't heard after all, but then she saw that
he had paled beneath his heavy tan and was standing
very still.

'Crikey!' he muttered, his expression appalled. 'I've
just realised I left the first-aid kit under the seat in the
van.'

Jancy sank to sit on a wet rock, near to tears, while
Cliff struggled to get back his professionalism. 'Not to
worry,' he said eventually, his cheerfulness forced.

'Only a couple more hours till we reach the hut at Dead Man's Falls. There'll be all sorts of first-aid stuff there.'

The name of the falls was unfortunate. Jancy looked as if it might have to be changed to Dead Woman's Falls before the day was out. . .or possibly Murdered Tour Leader's Falls. Thea could sympathise. Nothing was worse than trying to hike with a heavy pack when your head throbbed and pounded at every step.

'I've got what you need, Jancy, don't worry,' Joe came in, to everyone's unspoken relief. 'It's paracetamol so it won't upset your stomach as aspirin might have done. Here.'

He had already unshouldered his pack and was reaching into a side-pocket, which Thea could see contained a small but very practical cache of first-aid supplies. He shook two white pills into his hand and then said with a bit of impatience, 'Cliff, why don't you pour a mug of water to help her get them down?'

Jancy swallowed the pills gratefully while the others watched. She clearly needed several more minutes of rest, and Cathy said sensibly, 'I'll try and catch up to the others and tell them what's happened. They haven't realised we've stopped and they'll get way ahead if we're not careful.'

'Thanks, Cathy,' Cliff murmured, still clearly anxious and self-critical about his mistake over the first-aid kit.

Cathy set off gamely, after pushing damp dark hair off her forehead, and Thea watched the small form disappear around a shaded curve in the track some distance ahead, to flash into view again every now and then as an ever-shrinking dot of bright red and blue. Jancy still didn't seem ready to move on, although another group of four trampers had now overtaken them.

'You'll love the hut,' Cliff said with manufactured

enthusiasm. 'It was modernised four years ago and it's really luxurious. You can hear the falls all night, too. Most people say it's one of the best night's sleep they've ever had.'

'And you're planning a proper break in about fifteen minutes, aren't you?' Joe prompted the tour leader, seeing that the promise of the hut was still too far distant to appeal to Jancy.

'Yes. Right.' Cliff took his cue awkwardly. 'We'll have some more nuts and chocolate and people can put down their packs for ten minutes or so.'

Without speaking Jancy got up, reaching her hand to Peter, who helped her as she grunted with effort. The group of five set off, with Jancy and Peter in the lead, Cliff in between and Joe and Thea following closely behind. Noting the way Joe watched the chubby, tired figure ahead, Thea guessed that he had slowed his own pace deliberately in order to keep close at hand in case there was a further problem, and she was determined to keep here with Joe at the rear of the party herself, as her confidence in Cliff's leadership has been rather shaken.

For a good while, all went well. Jancy announced as they enjoyed the promised snack and rest that her headache had gone, and the fact that they didn't catch up to the rest of the group was probably a good thing: it meant that the faster walkers were making their way steadily on towards Dead Man's Falls without mishap.

Then, at four o'clock, the rearguard of five reached Daley's River.

'This is a magnificent spot!' Cliff enthused as a narrow swing bridge came into view ahead. 'The bridge is a hundred and twenty feet above the rapids, but often you can still feel the spray and mist cooling your legs.'

'A hundred and twenty feet! And it's another swing bridge! Great!' Jancy said thinly.

This wasn't the first such bridge they had crossed today, but it was easily the highest and longest. Thea had a healthy respect for heights but no real fear of them, so she waited quite calmly for Jancy to step gingerly in Peter's wake on to the bouncing curve of planks and metal meshing. Cliff and Joe started forward as well, and Thea brought up the rear, planning to enjoy the view of the foaming torrent below.

Actually, it was harder than it looked. Droplets of mist from the river had made the boards slippery, and, even though there was raised wooden beading under-foot every few steps and a sturdy wire cable to hold on to with each hand, with a heavy pack it was slow, uncertain going. Thea sensibly decided to enjoy the view when she got to the other side.

Meanwhile Jancy inched forward. The reluctant young woman didn't realise that a quicker, more rhythmic pace actually would have made things easier than her nervous shuffle, and an impatient exclamation from Peter a third of the way across didn't help.

Then, disaster struck. One minute they were going well. Jancy was even picking up her pace a little. Next minute there came a terrified scream, the bridge bounced wildly and Jancy fell to her knees, twisting her body crookedly as the pack threatened to slide off and wedge itself against the mesh sides of the bridge.

But at first Jancy didn't care about her pack or her fall. 'A spider!' she screamed. 'A huge spider! *Huge*!'

Peter dropped his own pack and hurried back to her, making the bridge bounce giddily again. 'It's gone, Jancy. The spider's gone.' Then his tone of reassurance changed to alarm. 'But your leg!'

Jancy looked down and Cliff, who had dropped his pack on to the planks as sell, said sharply, 'What's wrong?'

'She's gashed her leg. There was a loose board and
. . .look, there's a nail sticking out of it.'

'Oh, lord, and the first-aid kit is ——'

'She's going to faint.' Joe's voice was a sharp,
authoritative crack and Peter, swearing under her
breath, lunged forward and clutched Jancy before she
subsided against the mesh. Between the wire and the
planks there was a six-inch gap—not enough to fall
through but a little giddying none the less.

'I don't understand,' Peter was saying fuzzily. 'She's
a bit iffy about heights but not usually like this.'

'It's not the height, it's the blood,' Joe said crisply.

He had already taken a Swiss army knife and a clean
handkerchief from his pocket and was kneeling beside
Jancy, his pack joining the growing pile on the plank
bridge. Deftly, he sliced an inch-wide strip from the
handkerchief.

'I'm bleeding,' Jancy moaned faintly.

'Don't look at it,' offered Peter. 'Look at. . .at the
view.'

Jancy looked down at the torrent of water gushing a
hundred and twenty feet below and moaned again.

'Here Jancy,' said Joe suddenly. 'Take my watch. I
need to get an idea of your—er—systolic blood
rhythm. Count for me. Every five seconds. Five. . .ten
. . .like thaat, OK? Got it? It's important.'

'Yes, I've got it,' Jancy said. 'Five. . .ten. . .
fifteen. . .'

She went on counting steadily and obediently, studying the watch face, and the thin red second hand with
an intent expression. Her colour slowly began to
improve. Joe began to wrap the large section of handkerchief firmly around the gashed leg, which was
bleeding quite heavily.

'Could I get that bandage out of your pack?' Thea

offered, and felt rebuked when he only shook his head impatiently.

'The spider. . .' Jancy said now, breaking off her counting rhythm and sounding out of control once more. 'Where has it gone?'

'It's well away,' Joe answered firmly. 'I saw it running back along the wire towards the other side.'

Thea caught his imploring glance and she realised why. The spider — and it certainly was a large one — was actually sitting on the wire cable just above Jancy's left shoulder. Not being particularly fond of spiders herself, especially hairy ones like this, Thea needed all her courage to answer the unspoken request in Joe's eyes: Get that spider out of here!

Carefully she took off her white cotton hat and muttered something incomprehensible about going back to see if any other hikers were approaching, then she wrapped the hat around the spider and the cable and shook the latter, hoping the creature would drop safely into the hat's crown. It did. Scrunching up the brim to form a sort of bag from which the hairy thing could not possibly escape. . .and *crawl* on to her. . . Thea hurried back along the bridge and flung the unspeakable arachnid into the undergrowth. Whew!

Back at the group gathered around Jancy, she found that Joe had secured his makeshift bandage in place with the thin side-strip he had cut from the handkerchief. Jancy was still counting.

'Can you get up now?' the doctor said to her gently.

'I. . . I think so.'

'Good. When we get safely off the bridge and find a spot with clear running water I'll wash that cut and bind it up properly with gauze bandage and antiseptic cream.'

Thea realised now why he hadn't wanted her to get out the proper bandage at once. He hadn't wanted to waste it on a cut that hadn't yet been washed. In other words, he only had one length of gauze. She hoped that the warden at Dead Man's Falls was prepared to part with some first-aid supplies for the rest of the journey.

'Cliff, take her pack, would you?' Joe was saying now, again a little impatiently.

Cliff had betrayed helplessness again during the drama over Jancy's fall, and, while it was obvious that he was angry with himself, this didn't help anyone at all. Taking the injured woman's pack seemed to help the tour leader. He gritted his teeth and swung his own very heavy pack on to his left shoulder, using just one of the straps, then stood still while Peter helped him lift Jancy's pack on to his right shoulder. Peter had his pack on now and was gently pushing Jancy in front of him with both hands reassuringly touching her back. She limped but went faster now that the far bank was approaching.

Cliff let the two of them get well ahead then turned to Joe, his face still pale and twisted into a grimace of anxiety. 'I've really messed this up, haven't I?' he began.

'Don't waste time on self-reproach,' Joe answered. 'Just get off this bridge! You're carrying two packs!'

'Oh, I can manage that,' Cliff laughed harshly. 'I'm fit, at least. Crikey, I've got to tell you! This is my first tour, and I don't know what I'm doing.'

'Yes, I guessed it was your first,' Joe nodded calmly, but Thea was thinking in a mild panic, His first! No wonder! Help! And thank goodness Joe is here!

'I've been tramping these tracks for years. I'm fit, I can fix a broken-down car, I know about the wildlife, and I came through the training course that the tour company gave us with no trouble. But ——'

'There's a first time for everything,' Joe said, his low

voice making the words sincere and supportive. 'Don't worry. What you've been telling us about the plant and animal life around here and the history of the region has been great. As for messing things up. . .if you want my advice——'

'Anything!'

'—just think about your group and who they are,' Joe said, his mouth held soberly. He was looking steadily at Cliff with his intelligent yet warm blue eyes. Thea saw the mist of sweat that clung to his throat and temples and realised that he had had to make an effort not to be angry with the tour leader. 'Try and see all this from their perspective and you'll do better,' he went on. 'It's what I try to remind myself in medicine: Think like a patient. On your next tour, they'll all think you've been doing it for years.'

'If there *is* a next tour,' Cliff retorted bitterly.

'Just get off this bridge, will you?' Joe came in, half laughing, half serious. It was getting late now and they still had a kilometre more to walk to reach the hut. With Jancy slowing their pace and her leg to dress properly as soon as possible, time was getting tight.

Obediently, Cliff started off, carrying the two bouncing packs as if they were school lunch bags. Thea, just ahead of Joe now, said what she had been wanting to say for the last ten minutes, '*Systolic blood rhythm*? Is that a medical discovery of your own?'

Joe grinned sheepishly, his mouth creasing at the corners. 'It just came out,' he said. 'I almost tried "pulmonic spasm rate" but that sounded a bit scary. The only point was to get her to keep looking at that watch, not at the blood or the spider or those yawning yards of empty air. But come on, let's pick up the pace.'

It was half-past six by the time they all straggled up to the hut.

\* \* \*

The moon was full. It shone blue and white on Mount Aspiring dreaming in the distance, its glistening pyramid shape punctuating a long, lush valley that led upwards to a vista of maze-like glaciers and ridges. The rushing falls nearby, also white and shining in the moonlight, reminded Thea of the icy dip she had taken before dinner just downstream of the main cascade.

The frigid snow-melt had washed away both grime and weariness, leaving her ravenous for the meal of spaghetti and meaty tomato sauce that tonight's cooking team had prepared. Her own team had been responsible for the washing-up tonight, and now that it was all done some people had gathered around a table for cards, one or two were reading, while others chatted with the other two parties of trampers who occupied this twenty-six-bed hut.

Thea didn't feel like doing any of those things. The hut seemed a little stuffy after the fresh outdoor day, and the lingering smell of spaghetti and soup in the air was no longer appetising now that she had eaten her fill. Out here it had chilled considerably since the sun had dropped below the western mountains, but in her pullover and wind-jacket, with shorts exchanged again for sturdy jeans, she didn't feel at all cold.

Not wanting to stray too far from the hut, she found a flat rock on the edge of a grassy clearing and sat down, content simply to watch the stars. As it happened, the rock she had chosen — had she chosen it deliberately? — was big enough for two, and somehow she wasn't surprised when Joe Stockwell joined her a few minutes later, his eyes very dark and his teeth glinting whitely as he broke into his slow thoughtful smile.

'Mind?' he said briefly as he dropped down beside her.

'Of course not.'

They didn't say anything more. It wasn't necessary. The evening was better without words. Then, after a timeless interval, his arm came around her, reassuring in its plaid flannel sleeve, and he said, very carefully and very low, 'Is it too soon to kiss you?'

'No. . .' Willingly and with heat rising in her like warm bread, she turned into his arms and tilted her face.

His lips quested unhurriedly as if he were exploring the taste and feel of her skin in great detail. They were smooth, firm lips — warm and dry, too. After making a hot, tingling trail across her jaw he finally parted her mouth and she began an exploration that was as searching and delicious as his. Her hands ran along the soft flannel of his shirt, finding the rippled shape of the muscles she knew would be there.

He caressed her shoulders, soothing away a tenderness left by the straps of her heavy pack. Their noses bumped gently together and she was enveloped in the scent of him — a mixture of soap, woodsmoke and maleness that was tangy and delightful and new. It was a long time before he pulled reluctantly away from her . . .not very far away, just enough to look at her in the moonlight.

She looked at him as well — at the steady eyes, at the high, intelligent forehead that so often had a lock or two of red-glinted brown hair falling over it, at the careless scattering of freckles over the bridge of his well-defined nose. But each of them saw much more than these small physical details. They saw a potential future that was wonderful and frightening as well.

'Thea, is this too good to be true?' he murmured finally, in the low, resonant voice that she was quickly growing to love.

'Oh, I hope not. . .' she answered softly, and tilted her face once more to receive his kiss.

\* \* \*

'I can't believe these three weeks have gone so fast!'
Jancy exclaimed, poised to bite into a hot slice of toast
and take a gulp of breakfast coffee. It was the last
morning of the tour, and they would arrive back at the
tour's hotel base in Christchurch by late afternoon.

Tanned and a little slimmer now, Jancy looked much
happier than she had done when the tour began. The
ugly tear on her leg was almost healed, thanks to Joe
Stockwell's continued attention.

'It really could have done with a stitch or two,' he
had confessed to Thea. 'But by the time we got back
to civilisation it was too late for that.'

Only Thea really understood how carefully Joe had
watched for signs of infection and how meticulous he
had been about dressing the injury and treating it with
antiseptic powder or cream. Dr Stockwell wasn't the
sort of man to draw attention to the extra efforts he
made. It was one of the things she loved about him.

How strange. . .and wonderful. . .and frightening
. . .to think that she could use the word 'love' about
Joe when she had known him such a short time! She
hadn't said the word aloud yet, not to Joe or anybody
else, but she was sure of it all the same, and she was
*almost* as sure that Joe felt it just as strongly.

They had spent almost every waking minute together
since that night at Dead Man's Falls. Part of the time,
very privately, they had continued their sensual exploration of one another but mostly they had been too
busy for that, hiking, talking, doing camp duties, taking
pictures, chatting with the other tour members.

Strangely enough, it was all these very ordinary
things that told Thea she loved Joe. Those heady
moments under the moonlight were all very well. . .
and very wonderful. . .but such things could be deceptive. Sharing their awed contemplation of a stunning
view, laughing till the tears came over a campfire joke,

telling each other about plans and ambitions as they washed the dishes outdoors in the sunset. . .those were the things that proved it all meant something.

'What's everyone doing after this?' Jancy continued with cheerful curiosity. 'Let's not all lose touch! Joe, are you going straight back to Sydney?'

'No.' He shook his head. 'My brother and a couple of mates are flying in tomorrow evening and we've got three more weeks of hiking planned. The Heaphy track first, then up to Abel Tasman National Park and the North Island.'

'And after that?'

'Back to Sydney. By then I'll have heard where I'll be working this year. I've applied for several places. Mainly in country districts on the coast.'

'In hospitals?'

'No, general practice. Partnerships, sometimes on call and with visiting rights at the local hospital.'

'Sounds good,' Jancy concluded.

'Hope so,' he agreed laconically.

Thea hadn't said anything during this. She knew it all already, of course. Last night they had discussed it very seriously. 'I've always wanted to work in the country somewhere,' Joe had said. 'A place where there is good camping and hiking to be done, and near the coast as well, preferably. But with you being in Sydney. . .somehow Byron Bay and Coffs Harbour and Grafton have lost their appeal a bit.'

'Well,' Thea had answered hesitantly, 'I'm not saying I'll always be in Sydney. There's room for change in my life.'

'Good. . .'

It was the closest they had come to an open acknowledgement of their feelings for each other, but for the time being it was enough.

The spotlight had moved away from Joe now, as

other tour group people told of their plans. Several were making their way up to the North Island, including one rather sour couple whom Thea — and most of the others — had been finding increasingly irritating over the past three weeks. Jancy and Peter were headed north as well.

'Peter promised me we'd do the North Island in a *civilised* way,' the former said. 'Rent a car and stay in motels. As long as I put up with the camping bit first.'

'Has it been total torture?' Cliff put in slyly. He had loosened up, as had Jancy herself, after that first disastrous day on the Daley River track. Joe's advice had been the crucial thing Thea considered. She had caught Cliff more than once mouthing to himself, Think like a patient, and his understanding of people's feelings and concerns had improved visibly.

'No, it hasn't been torture at all,' Jancy responded — generously, since she had suffered with her leg on that first long hike. 'Milford Sound was fantastic, and Lake Te Anau, and the white-water-rafting trip. On Stewart Island the rain was a bit icky, but then we had that night on the town in Dunedin. . . No, I've had a great time.'

Joe and Thea exchanged a private glance and smile that said very clearly, Not as great as ours has been.

'We'd better get a move on, everyone,' Cliff announced. 'We have to clean the tents and the van ready for the next group, and I want to get you all into Christchurch by four.'

'I feel as if it's over already,' Cathy said a little sadly.

'Don't argue about it, Thea. I'm coming to the airport with you!' Joe Stockwell said, his blue eyes looking positively angry about the matter.

Thea answered helplessly, 'If you really want to. . .'

'Of *course* I want to!' He took a commanding pace

forward and gripped her arms. 'You're not suggesting
I'd have anything better to do, are you? We all got
used to getting up early on the tour and Richard and
the others aren't flying in to start our trip together till
late this afternoon. When's your taxi due?'

'In about five minutes.' It was six in the morning and
they stood outside Joe's room, talking in intense
whispers.

'And you were thinking we could say goodbye in five
minutes?'

'No, I was hoping you *would* come to the airport,
but——'

He laughed. 'Silly thing!' he said, and swept her up
into his arms to squeeze her slim waist and then push
the hair off her face so that he could kiss her. By the
time he finished doing so, they had to run to collect her
luggage from outside her room down the corridor,
clatter downstairs to the hotel foyer and dash to catch
the attention of the waiting taxi driver, who was on the
point of driving off in disgust.

On the way to the airport, there didn't seem to be
much to say. Thea listlessly studied the early morning
sights that rolled past the window, thinking that three
weeks was a horribly long time. Funny, that! The three
weeks just past seemed like a delightful morsel of
living, all too short. How could the twenty-one days
that lay ahead seem to stretch out inexorably?

Then, once they reached the terminal, which was
already well awake for the day, there was suddenly too
much to say and no time to say it in. Thea had to check
in at the airline counter, buy a promised souvenir for
her mother, change her remaining New Zealand cur-
rency into Australian dollars. . .and already the first
boarding announcement was being made. They began
to talk very fast at that point, their words tumbling on
top of each other.

'I wish I weren't going to the blasted North Island. . .'

'You've got my address. If you can't reach me there for any reason, you've got my mother's phone number, too.'

'I've memorised both of them!'

'But you should get me at the flat. . .'

'My flight gets in on the Tuesday morning.'

'Have a great time.'

'I'll send you postcards.'

'I've got to go. Don't I have to go through Customs?'

'Yes. . . Oh, damn!'

Thea had to gulp back tears. They kissed clumsily and she wanted to grab him with both hands and just hold him to her till the flight left and it was too late, but she didn't and after a minute he thrust her away with gritted teeth as if *he* had wanted her to miss the plane as well.

'Thea?'

'Yes?'

'I. . .' He hesitated and in the air between them she could almost hear the words that she wanted but didn't dare to say herself. I love you. Would he say it? 'I. . . I can't wait to see you again.'

'Neither can I.'

And then he pushed her towards the doors with the sign above them reading 'Passengers only beyond this point'. One rough, tanned hand pulled her face to his one last time and seconds later, without her quite knowing how it had happened, she was through the door and he had gone from sight.

# CHAPTER THREE

HOT needles of refreshing water coursed over Thea's body, renewing her after the early start to the day and the three-hour flight. In Sydney she had collected her luggage, cleared Customs quickly and taken a taxi straight home to the flat, so it was still barely nine in the morning, Sydney time.

It was probably silly to have a shower before even starting to unpack the travel-stained belongings from her backpack. In fact, the pack sat in a remote corner of the living-room floor where she had unceremoniously dumped it and she felt more inclined to take a snooze after this shower than to tackle its contents. She and Joe had stayed up too late last night, talking.

Joe. . . As the water caressed her skin, Thea thought of how he had caressed her with such tender expertise. He was over a thousand miles away now, and she felt such a mixture of happiness and misery when she thought about him that it exhausted her. Miserable at not seeing him for three weeks, of course, but utterly happy because being with him felt so right.

Well, she couldn't stay in the shower forever. Sighing happily as another image of Joe came to her — his body streaming with water as he rose joyously from a dip in the cold, sparkling river they had rafted down — Thea seized a towel, dried herself vigorously, wrapped the big pink sheet of towelling around herself and stepped out into the small bathroom. . .

To greet a nightmare.

An attractive, dark-haired woman in her late thirties stood there and at first Thea was too bewildered to

recognise her. The storm of angry emotional words
that the woman unleashed on Thea's head didn't help
her to come to grips with the situation either.

'Where's Ewan? Don't tell me he isn't here because
I know he is. I've been a fool about this but I won't be
one any longer. . .'

It was the director of nursing at Mount Royal
Hospital, Thea finally realised. Trish Baxter. Someone
whom Thea had always liked. The angry, bitter words
continued for some seconds, giving Thea, who was
utterly speechless, the chance to realise that the director of nursing was upset as well as angry. Her hair was
untidy as if she had forgotten to brush it this morning,
her mauve and white spotted blouse was tucked crookedly into a dark skirt and, most telling of all, her eyes
were reddened and her nose puffed up from a long
session of crying.

'Well, what have you got to say for yourself?' she
demanded at last, her voice cracking, but Thea, feeling
vulnerable, half angry, half sympathetic and utterly
confused, didn't have anything to say at all.

What could this possibly be about? Mrs Baxter had
mentioned her husband Ewan. . . And suddenly there
he was, Dr Ewan Baxter, orthopaedic surgeon, standing in the doorway of Charmaine's bedroom, his dark
trousers pulled hastily and untidily up to his waist so
that they revealed an inch of purple and black leopard-
spotted underwear on one side. His upper body, which
was broad and too thickly muscled, was bare, his hair
was rumpled and his eyes were very bleary. Behind
him, Charmaine's room was empty.

Thea gasped at the sight of the surgeon and Trish
Baxter shot her a furious and triumphant glance,
evidently taking her expression of shocked and growing
understanding as one of guilt.

'At least it's out in the open now,' the director of

nursing hissed at Thea. 'How you can have had the gall
to send me a *Christmas* card this year. . . Oh, my God!'
She suddenly buried her face in her hands and began
to sob.

Thea's instinct, even in the midst of this ghastly
mess, was to comfort her in some way, but of course it
was impossible. Instead, she glared at Ewan Baxter —
she had never liked him! — until he was forced to speak.

'Let's deal with this in some dignity, shall we,
Patricia?' he said in a voice of iron control.

'Ewan. . .?' His wife looked up at him, stifling her
tears.

'Wait while I get my shirt.' He disappeared back into
the bedroom.

'This isn't. . . I've been away on holiday in——'
Thea broke off. Trish Baxter's look was glacial.

Seconds later Dr Baxter emerged again, buttoning a
pin-striped shirt. 'Come on, Trish. We have to talk.
But not now. I was due at the hospital half an hour ago
and I'm sure you're running late as well.'

'Does it matter?' the director of nursing said, trying
to match his control. 'Isn't this more important?'

'Darling, I've got surgery at ten-thirty and an important case conference before that.'

Coolly, he opened the front door of the flat, ushering
his wife out and letting the door shut behind him.

Thea's heart was racing and she felt hot all over. It
was as if a tornado had just passed through her life and
now she was left numb and breathless, trying to pick
up the pieces. Automatically she went to her room to
find clothes, since she was still draped in her damp
towel and feeling very vulnerable that way. The room
was just as she had left it — the bed made up with its
Wedgwood-green and white spread, and shelves, dressing-table and chest of drawers all neat as a pin.

With personal belongings such as her brush and

comb still in her backpack, the room looked unoccupied, like a spare room. The fact that it was the smaller of the two bedrooms in the flat only added to this impression and, realising this, Thea at last began to have a clearer idea of what was going on.

Charmaine was having an affair with Ewan Baxter! They must have spent the night together, and then Charmaine had left for an early shift at the hospital. Trish Baxter must have found the spare key to the flat that Charmaine had given Ewan. Thea remembered now how the key had disappeared mysteriously several weeks ago. Charmaine had shrugged when asked about it, but. . .

And the key had a hospital tag on it, as well as the phone number of the flat! Somehow the director of nursing had managed some detective work and had arrived at the correct address.

I've got to explain! was Thea's first wild thought. Now! I'll get dressed and—— She began to dress feverishly, pulling out underwear, flared floral dress shorts and a matching blouse and diving hastily into them. Before the blouse was buttoned, though, she realised that her plan could not work. She couldn't just go to the office of the director of nursing and say to her, Excuse me, I've been away in New Zealand. Actually, it's my flatmate Charmaine who's ruining your marriage, not me.

Thea, like most Australians, had a healthy horror of telling tales, or 'dobbing on' someone, as schoolchildren called it nowadays. Also, her story would not sound very convincing, she realised, seeing the scene as it must have looked to Trish: Thea emerging nearly naked from the shower, Ewan emerging nearly naked from the bedroom and no one else in sight.

Dressed now, she went to the living-room to search out brush and comb from her backpack to tidy her freshly washed hair. Charmaine's shift would end at three. Hopefully, she would be home by half-past three. They could talk it out. . .

Not considering what she hoped Charmaine would say, Thea waited out the long day. She unpacked and did her laundry, then went out and bought some provisions for the flat as Charmaine had let the inventory get rather low over the past three weeks. After lunch she tried to have a nap, as her day had started so early, but she found that she was too churned up to sleep.

By five she realised that Charmaine wasn't coming home, and with a pang of guilt remembered that she hadn't even phoned her mother to say that she was safely back.

'You *are* coming to dinner, aren't you?' Mrs Carmichael asked anxiously, and hastily Thea said that yes, of course she was.

'David wants to come and pick you up on his motorbike. . .' Pamela Carmichael went on in a tone that betrayed both anxiety and disapproval.

'Tell him I'd love it,' Thea responded firmly, and half an hour later David was at her door with a spare helmet in his hand. Charmaine had still not returned to the flat.

'This'll sweep away the cobwebs,' her younger brother said cheerfully, shaking untidy light brown hair out of his eyes. He was tall, and still in the gangly stage, but two or three years from now he would be a good-looking young man, Thea realised proudly.

'What cobwebs?' she answered him with spirit. 'I've just spent three weeks in the wilds of New Zealand where there isn't a cobweb in sight.'

'OK, well, no need for me to go fast, in that case.'

'No, no need at all,' Thea answered very firmly.

'You don't want to end up like some of the people I saw when I worked on Casualty last year.'

'Actually, I've just had a bit of a prang,' he admitted as they reached the waiting bike and strapped helmets into place.

'No!'

'Oh, it was nothing.' He was a little defensive now. 'I took a turn too widely and knocked over a mailbox. Had to get the front wheel realigned — don't know what they did to fix the mailbox! — but I wasn't hurt.'

'Thank goodness.'

'Just wanted to tell you because Mum won't leave the subject alone.'

'Hmm.'

David revved his engine and it became too noisy to say anything more. In any case, Thea knew she had said enough. Put off by his mother's tendency to go on and on, David needed short, pithy lectures if lectures were to be given at all.

Settling down to the ride, Thea found she enjoyed it more than she had expected to. David *wasn't* a reckless driver, she was relieved to discover, although he was still definitely an inexperienced one. Fortunately he seemed to realise this and was, if anything, over-cautious at the busiest intersections.

In short, they arrived safely. 'You're here! I've been so worried. . . Thank goodness you had no mishaps!' was Pamela Carmichael's greeting. Her eyes were wide and her movements rapid and nervous.

'Oh, there were some hairy moments,' Thea replied, thinking of New Zealand and that swing bridge where Jancy had fallen. 'But no major disasters.'

'What do you mean "no major disasters"?' Her mother was aghast at once. 'There were some *minor* disasters, then? David, you didn't ——'

'I was talking about New Zealand,' Thea came in quickly. 'David drove beautifully.'

'But he told you about——'

'Yes, but it sounds like a mistake in steering that he's already learnt from.'

'Don't tell anyone, though, will you? Especially Grand——'

'No, I won't. . .' Suppressing a sigh, Thea quickly rummaged in her bag to find the souvenirs she had brought.

'Thea. Won't be home tonight. Love Charmaine,' Thea read aloud later that night when she found the note propped up on the kitchen table at the flat. It was written on pink paper and Charmaine had, as usual, made the dot over the 'i' in her name in the form of a tiny heart.

Yuck! How *twee*! Thea thought angrily, though the harmless if rather childish gimmick had never particularly bothered her before.

The fact was, she was getting more and more angry with Charmaine by the minute. Dinner at her mother's had been fairly pleasant, with so much to tell about New Zealand. . .nothing about Joe Stockwell just yet, though. . .but on the way home, again on the back of David's bike, Thea had felt a headache tightening its grip on her temples. Charmaine had better have the right things to say!

And now she wasn't here at all. Yet she must know by now that something was going on. Ewan must have spoken to her during the day. The thing between the two of them hadn't just been a one-night stand, Thea was sure of that. Dr Baxter had been far too thoroughly in control. Thea had the feeling that he was extremely at home in the flat: she had found a brand of beer in the fridge that she had never even heard of before, and

masculine shaving cream in the bathroom. Even someone as unsophisticated as she was knew what that sort
of thing meant.

With little choice other than to go to bed, Thea did
so. Work started again tomorrow — an early shift. She
couldn't sleep, though. After about an hour she heard
the low vibration of thunder and soon heavy summer
rain was drumming outside so loudly it seemed the
storm had actually burst over her head. Apt, somehow.
February could be a stormy month in Sydney.

'There's a message for you, Thea,' said Gail Reed, a
fellow nurse on Bryant Medical Ward, the next day.

Thea nodded and took the slip of paper Gail held
out. It was two o'clock in the afternoon and after a
restless night and an early start — and still no word
from Charmaine — Thea was very ready to go home in
an hour's time. She should be finished promptly at
three. . .

Not today, it seemed. The message was a bland
summons to the office of the director of nursing, as
soon as she was released from duty.

To apologise? Thea hoped fervently. Perhaps
Charmaine had been to see Mrs Baxter, or Ewan had
explained.

Evidently not. Alone with the director of nursing an
hour later, Thea had no difficulty in perceiving her
anger. Trish Baxter was neatly dressed today and her
make-up, heavier than usual, was very carefully
applied, but she looked tired and miserable and ready
to fly apart at the slightest thing.

Poor woman! Thea thought. The director of nursing
had been so nice in the past, and the Christmas card
that Thea had impulsively sent seven weeks ago had
been prompted by the woman's help with a tricky
problem of protocol on the ward. Today, though, Trish
Baxter's dark eyes were like cold stones and her white

teeth seemed ready to emit electric sparks when she opened her mouth to speak.

'You are dismissed from the hospital, Sister Carmichael, and that dismissal is effective immediately,' the dark-haired woman said without preamble. 'I'm sure it's what you yourself will decide is best.' The word came out as a hiss, followed by a raggedly drawn breath. 'In fact, I'm prepared to accept your resignation, since that will look better when you apply for future jobs than if I had simply sacked you.'

She paused, and Thea murmured an awkward, 'Thank you'.

'Don't you have anything else to say?' Trish Baxter demanded through a tight throat.

Do I? Thea wondered to herself desperately. I *must* see Charmaine. She's got to see what a hole I'm in! Aloud, she answered weakly, 'Um—not yet. I—I hope you'll soon see that perhaps things aren't quite as they seem.'

The director of nursing gave a harsh laugh. 'Oh, for God's sake! Are you going to tell me that my husband *hasn't* been unfaithful at all?'

'No, but——'

'Just get out, will you?'

Thea did so, arriving in the bland hospital corridor outside Mrs Baxter's office almost giddy with dismay. I *must* find Charmaine *now*! If she's on an afternoon shift. . .

Making her way quickly up to the orthopaedic ward on the fifth floor, Thea soon found her flatmate at the nurses' station working on reports. 'We have to talk,' she whispered urgently in a low tone over the raised bench-top to the willowy redhead.

'Oh, hi, Thea,' Charmaine said smoothly, her lips opening in a brief, insincere smile. 'How was New Zealand? Meet anyone interesting?'

I'm not going to tell her about Joe, Thea thought, her teeth gritted. Dr Joe Stockwell, probably hiking the Heaphy track with his brother Richard at this very moment, seemed achingly far away. Suppressing the familiar image of him in T-shirt and backpack, she said through her teeth, 'I haven't come for a chat. Where can we go?'

'Ward conference room's bound to be free at this hour,' Charmaine returned easily, and with a glance at the ward sister, whose back was turned, she slipped away from her desk and went with Thea. 'What's this about, then?'

'You *must* know!' Thea burst out.

The door of the ward conference room was safely shut between them and the rest of the ward, and Thea began to tell Charmaine what had happened. 'And you *must* go and see Trish Baxter yourself before this goes any further,' she concluded. 'I know it must be difficult for you. . .' She softened her tone, trying valiantly to see the issue from her flatmate's point of view — perhaps Ewan Baxter had seduced Charmaine into the whole thing and she didn't know how to get out of it. She went on, 'Mrs Baxter just had me down to her office and told me she'd *let* me resign instead of sacking me straight out.'

Suddenly Charmaine dropped her pretence of ignorance and her eyes narrowed in accusation. 'So of course you told her the way it really was?'

'Of *course* I didn't!' Thea returned indignantly. 'It's up to you to do that. It's your. . .affair, after all.' She chose the word deliberately. 'Only please do it *soon*, or this business of my losing my job will start to grind through the system and it could take weeks to——'

'You mean she still thinks it's you?'

'Yes, and——' Thea stopped as she saw the slow,

satisfied smile that sneaked on to Charmaine's long, rather pale face.

'Oops,' Charmaine said, her tone flippant and her smile crooked and cynical now.

Light dawned on Thea at last, and she whispered, horrified, 'You mean you're not going to tell Trish Baxter the truth?'

Charmaine shrugged and tossed a lock of dark red hair off her forehead. She spread her hands apologetically, as if the whole thing were really beyond her control. 'I'd better get back to work,' she said, then, faced with the naked, despising look that Thea couldn't help giving her, she added, the façade suddenly breaking, 'Don't you see, Dorothea Carmichael, you naïve little idiot? I love the man and I've *got* to get him to leave that woman and come to me! He's on the point of it. . . I know he is. . .but he's not there yet. Ewan would never forgive me for creating a huge scandal at the hospital, but if Trish and everyone else thinks that it's *you*, and you've gone, then I've got a chance.'

'At my expense.' Even now, Thea could scarcely believe the rationalisation she was hearing.

'All's fair in love and war,' Charmaine crowed harshly, then lowered her voice to a passionate hiss once more. 'You don't understand! When have you ever been in love? Ewan Baxter is everything I want in a man. He's got sophistication, a great body, and money, and I'm *not* going to risk losing him for the sake of some stupid little nursing friendship. If you were in my position you'd do the same in a second.'

With this, she whirled around, seized the door and wrenched it open, her feet then sounding a rapid rhythm on the polished linoleum floor in the corridor outside.

Numbly, Thea followed her from the room and took a side-corridor that led to the little-frequented stairs.

She couldn't face *anybody* at this moment. Her options listed themselves one after the other in her mind: Go back to Trish Baxter, go to the head of hospital personnel, go to Ewan Baxter himself. . .

But she rejected each of these as impossible. The director of nursing would not believe her now without proof, the head of personnel would tell her it was a personal matter and not his affair — with the implication that it must be her fault in part, whatever the story was — and Ewan Baxter. . . With a shudder she thought of the man's handsome but rather cruel mouth and his expert way with words that could make even a senior nurse shrivel — and he liked to make them shrivel, too. If he, like Charmaine, saw it as an advantage that Trish had got the whole thing wrong. . .

Scarcely aware of her surroundings, she left the hospital and caught the bus back to her flat, the realisation growing that she really had lost her job and her flat as well. She wouldn't stay in this place another night, and she wouldn't even feel guilty that Charmaine's name was on the lease and she would be stuck with the rent. Probably Ewan Baxter would step in and cover the difference for her! The whole thing was so hideous that she no longer even wanted to find a way to stay at the hospital.

She began packing at once, using the empty boxes she still had stored away from her move here a year ago. In her anger and turmoil, the task didn't take long. The furniture belonged to the flat. All she had were four boxes of kitchen things and linen, her modest wardrobe, a carton or two of books and a couple more of ornaments and miscellaneous items. Once it was done, at a little after seven, she recklessly summoned a taxi and had the driver load everything in. Home to her mother's. It was the only thing to do.

Pamela Carmichael was appalled, of course, fussing,

wailing, wringing her hands. . .and demanding a detailed explanation.

'I can't,' answered Thea flatly, dumping a box in her old bedroom and returning to the front hall to pick up another. 'I had to leave, that's all, or. . .or it would have turned into a scandal that brought in the Carmichael name. You know how Grandpa would react to that. So don't make me say any more. This way, it can all be forgotten.'

The fear that if Thea talked about it, even to her mother, Grandfather Carmichael might become involved was enough to silence Pamela Thea, and after a hasty meal of eggs that she did not even taste Thea retired early to bed to sleep the sleep of someone who was physically and emotionally exhausted.

A train clattered its way through the lush, dairy-lands of the New South Wales South Coast region, bearing Thea towards the interview with Grandfather Carmichael that she had hastily set up that morning. To the right of the train rose a rugged escarpment that shadowed ancient temperate rainforests, while to the left there were glimpses of sparkling blue-green ocean.

Normally Thea loved the journey down to her grandparents', and loved the whole South Coast region as well, but today she was rather blind to beauty. Was she doing the right thing? The idea had suggested itself to her amid yesterday's turmoil, and this morning, waking refreshed, she had found that she had thoroughly decided to do it, without quite knowing how the decision had come about. Of course the whole thing might yet come to nothing. Grandpa might not be able to help her find a job away from Sydney at such short notice at all. He and Grandma Carmichael were going to Europe in a few days, she remembered. . . But she had to ask.

What about Joe? a small painful voice inside her kept saying. Two days ago she might have responded to the voice, and waited in Sydney doing nothing about her future until he returned and they could talk, but she was more wary now. Learning at first hand from Charmaine what deceit there could be in affairs of the heart, and what underhand things could be done in the name of love, she had begun to doubt those three weeks in New Zealand a little. After all, as Charmaine had so acidly pointed out, what did she know of love?

Perhaps for him it had only been a holiday romance. Perhaps new experiences were already overshadowing his memories of their time together and when he returned to Sydney in just under three weeks' time he would think to himself, That girl, Thea. . . Shall I phone her? Not just yet. And he would get caught up in moving away from Sydney to his new job and the phone call would never get made.

Stupid! Thea scolded herself, sniffing and wiping away several tears. She had pictured it all so vividly that she was acting as if it had already happened. I *will* wait. He's not like that. It *was* real for him; I won't make any commitments until I know where he's going to be.

But the doubts crept back in, and in the end her pride would not let her wait. I have to get on with my life, she realised. 'If it doesn't work out, and if I *have* just been waiting for him, I won't have any foundation left at all!'

Two hours later, after a bus ride through majestic, tangy forests of ribbon- and scribbly-gum, she had arrived in Tooma.

'Actually, as it happens, I can suggest you for a position,' Grandpa Carmichael told her half an hour later.

They sat together on a shady screened-in porch with

views of the dramatic, curved sweep of Conway Bay.
White-haired Mrs Carmichael was making a late lunch
for the three of them, and both Thea's grandparents
had been so pleased to see her that she had decided to
get the business of the trip over and done with straight-
away so that they could all enjoy the rest of the day
together walking on the beach towards Conway Point.

'You can?' Thea said, eagerness mixing crazily with
disappointment at her grandfather's response. If he
had been unable to help, she would have had an excuse
to dilly-dally till Joe came back.

'Yes, here at the hospital in Tooma. A vacancy has
suddenly opened up. Don't ask me to tell you why. A
rather unsettling sort of scandal.'

'A hospital scandal? Then I *don't* want to hear about
it!' said Thea, feeling only distaste and not a particle of
curiosity.

'Hmm,' Dr Carmichael narrowed his eyes shrewdly.
'That's not why *you're* suddenly interested in a change,
is it? You're not embroiled in ——'

'Yes, it *is* why,' Thea broke in frankly. 'And I *am*
embroiled! But through no fault of my own, and it's
absolutely horrid. I can tell you all about it if you like,
but. . .'

'Not now,' he soothed. 'I can see you don't want to,
and if you say you're not at fault then I believe you.
Perhaps later it might help to talk to us both about it.'

'Yes, it might at that,' she agreed, feeling a lot
better. Grandpa's unhesitating trust was balm to spirits
that had been sorely chafed over the past couple of
days.

'Now, about this job,' he said. 'It's only for three
months. After that, another nurse who has been on
extended maternity leave will be ready to come back.
I'll recommend you heartily, but there's a chance that
might not be enough. I'm chairman of the hospital

board, as you know, but the other board members might be a little chary of taking on a young, pretty nurse. After what has just happened at the hospital. . . Thea, if you *do* get the job. . .'

'Yes?'

'. . . there must be absolutely no question of getting romantically involved with *anyone* connected with the hospital. Do you understand what I'm saying and why?'

'Oh, yes!' she assured him fervently, thinking of Charmaine, Ewan and poor Trish Baxter. . .and thinking of Joe. 'I understand *exactly* what you're saying! Don't worry. There's no risk of that!'

'Aha! So you've decided that a doctor would make a poor husband, have you?' he teased.

Madly fighting off a blush, Thea could only murmur, 'Something like that.' Fortunately Grandpa seemed to be looking the other way.

Clutching Joe's postcard like a talisman, although she knew it practically off by heart, Thea stood waiting in the arrival concourse of Sydney airport's international terminal.

'I'd love it if you'd meet me at the airport,' Joe had written, on the back of a stunning view of Mount Egmont. 'But of course it's probably impossible. You'll be working. If by some lucky chance you can make it, here is my flight number and arrival time. . .'

Thea murmured these as she scanned the large board that showed all international arrivals. Yes, there it was: 'On time', and so was she. He should be coming through that nondescript door from Customs within the next ten minutes. . .

'Joe!'

'Thea!'

Heedless of his bags, he had swept her up off her feet and into his arms, nuzzling her with a face whose pleasant roughness betrayed the fact that he had not shaved in several days. Thea's heart was beating in her throat with painful happiness. He was just as she had remembered. . .better!

His grip on her was warm and solid and strong. The scent of him was fresh and outdoorsy and male. His eyes were blue and deep and steadfast. And those freckles on the bridge of his nose made her want to kiss it. . .and him. . .for minutes on end.

She *did* kiss him, not for minutes but for long, satisfying seconds that relaxed and warmed her as nothing else in the past difficult weeks had been able to do. His lips were as fresh and expert as she had remembered, making her own mouth swollen and hungry as she explored the taste and texture of him.

Releasing her at last, he grinned. 'Not at work?'

'Oh! No! Joe, I've got so much to tell you. . .'

'So have I. Here, if you can take this, I'll manage the rest.' He gave her two plastic bags of duty-free shopping, then shouldered his big pack and swung a small day-pack in one hand. 'How did you get out here?'

'My grandmother's car. I've got it for several months while my grandparents are overseas.'

'Then. . .can we go to my place?' He stopped and searched her face for a minute. 'Am I presuming too much here?'

'No. . .' she told him softly, and with an expression of very masculine satisfaction he wound his free arm through hers and squeezed her close to him.

'Thank God!' he said. 'I wasn't sure. I wondered if perhaps for you it had just been. . .'

'I know. I had the same doubts.'

Stopping helplessly, they kissed again in the middle of the car park.

'But I must tell you!' he said. 'I didn't want to say

anything in postcards. When Richard joined me he brought some letters, including one that. . . Well, to make it short, I've got a place in a partnership. The one I really wanted, too. I didn't even mention it to you before because I didn't want to jinx it. Superstitious, I know. . .'

'Where is it?' Thea asked, her heart in her mouth. Coffs Harbour? Byron Bay? Somewhere ten hours' drive from Tooma, where she was to start work at the community hospital on Monday. . .

'A great little town,' he answered. 'Near beautiful beaches but with fabulous hiking country all around——'

'For heaven's sake, Joe!'

'It's a general practice in a tiny place called Conway Bay, about four hours' drive from——'

'Conway Bay! Joe, that's three miles from Tooma Community Hospital, where Grandfather Carmichael has just helped me get a job. . .'

# CHAPTER FOUR

'WELL, we'll just have to keep the whole thing a secret.'

Thea's heart sank at Joe's easy words. She didn't know just what she had wanted him to say. . .but she knew it wasn't that. Secrecy! She had just told him the whole story of the new job, Grandpa's help, and his veto of any entanglement with hospital personnel. . . including visiting general practitioners. She had told Joe, too, all about why she needed the new job in the first place—about Charmaine and Ewan's affair, Trish Baxter's accusations, Charmaine's deceit.

He had been outraged on her behalf, of course. In the heat of the moment he had even offered to go and personally make mincemeat of the straying orthopaedic surgeon, and, if necessary, Ewan's new love as well. Then he had calmed down, pointed out that the whole thing was for the best, since now they would be living and working so close to one another, and hefted his backpack through the front door of the flat in Randwick that he shared with his brother Richard. It had taken the whole of the drive from the airport for the story to unfold.

And now he was calmly suggesting secrecy. At first it felt almost like a betrayal.

'I'm going to put the kettle on for you,' he was saying now. 'What would you like? Tea? Coffee?'

'Coffee, please.'

'Then I'm going to have a shower. I haven't had one for. . : I won't tell you how long,' he grinned. 'We've been roughing it. After that, I'll be able to kiss you properly.'

Nuzzling her nose briefly, he disappeared into a businesslike kitchen and clattered for some seconds with mug, kettle, spoon and coffee. Thea sat down on a comfortable grey couch and fiddled with a cushion while she waited. He couldn't know, of course, how much she hated secrecy and how it seemed to have plagued her all her life in the form of her mother's petty, anxious strictures.

True, he *did* understand how Charmaine's deceit had hurt her, and he would rightly suggest that what he was proposing would be very different from what Charmaine and Ewan had done. For one thing, there was no third person involved to be betrayed and wounded by it.

All the same, Thea could not shake off a sickening feeling of foreboding and reluctance. She could guess at some part of what would be involved—clandestine meetings, cryptic phone calls, a wariness about each outing they arranged. . . Joe passed by on his way to the shower, handing her a big mug of hot coffee. She summoned a smile; he kissed her. . .and noticed that something was amiss.

'Hey,' he said, teasing gently. 'It's only instant, and it's got long-life milk in it, but. . .is that the end of the world?'

'No.' She tried to smile again.

He guessed the problem. 'You don't like the idea of keeping this a secret, do you?'

'No, not really.'

He sat down beside her and she found that she didn't care how long it was since he had showered, she just wanted to feel his arms around her.

'Thea. . .' It was a hot whisper in her ear, then his lips grazed her face with light, teasing touches as he sought her mouth. His arms slipped around her shoulders and dropped to her waist, as if rediscovering her shape. She could feel his weight against her, warm, solid and strong. 'It was a secret in New Zealand, wasn't it?' he went on. 'We didn't flaunt it in front of everyone. Didn't fall on to picnic tables and start devouring each other, did we? I wanted to do that about ninety-seven per cent of the time, mind you. . .'

'That was different,' Thea said, her cheek pillowed on his shoulder and one hand exploring the springy texture of his dark brown hair. 'We didn't flaunt it, but we didn't have to lie. I think most people guessed by the end. Now we'll have to do everything we can to *prevent* people from guessing. I can see it, like some awful French bedroom farce, or something.'

He laughed softly at her expression and kissed a frown away. 'Not that bad, surely? I've never had any dark secrets to keep before, so I'm only guessing, but don't you think it might be rather fun?'

'Fun!'

'Don't spoil this with fears, Thea,' he whispered with sudden heat into her ear. 'All I'm thinking of at the moment is that we're a few minutes apart, instead of four hours or even more. What if I'd gone to Byron Bay? My entire salary would have been eaten up in petrol and air fares coming to see you every day I had off. I'd have had to ransom myself to a pyramid sales corporation to pay for it all. I'd end up trying to sell miracle soap and whizz-bang kitchen gadgets to my patients, and I'd get struck off the register for improper conduct. Then I'd go and——'

'Stop! Stop it!' She was laughing helplessly by now, her fears dissipated. He was so ridiculous! And it was so wonderful to hear that he had planned on spending all his free time with her. 'So when do you start?' she asked.

'Same week as you do.'

\*   \*   \*

'We only noticed them tonight at his bedtime when we couldn't get him to settle,' the anxious father told Thea, who was trying to examine the head of a crying toddler.

'Is he talking yet?' she asked.

'No, not really. Only a few words.'

'Hmm. I'm just wondering. . . Is there a song or rhyme game that he particularly loves? Because that might distract him enough for me to see. . .'

'Yes. Let me try. Um——' He launched into 'Incy Wincy Spider', which did quieten the little boy somewhat while Thea ran her fingers through the child's fine but rather dense hair and at last found what she was looking for — several hard round things like tiny dried lentils.

'Yes, they're ticks,' she told the father. 'Three or four of them.'

'I thought so. He's been fretful all day, but we just put it down to the touch of sun he got yesterday. Gee, what a disastrous holiday this is! Are they dangerous?'

'It's unlikely. Most of the ticks around here aren't,' Thea assured him.

It wasn't an area in which she had a lot of expertise, but there were some pamphlets about local creepy-crawlies in the front office of the Tooma community hospital, and Sister Joan Drummond, the director of nursing, had suggested she flip through them as soon as possible in case something like this cropped up.

And now it had, on her very first day. 'After we get them out, we'll pop them under a microscope just to check what kind they are,' Thea explained to Mr Evans.

Getting the creatures out wasn't as easy as her light tone had suggested. Mark Evans held little Alex while Thea attempted to fasten her tweezers to each pellet-like body. She knew that the best way was to take the insect by surprise and whisk it out before it had a chance to grip more tightly with its tiny but determined jaws. The trouble was, no sooner did she get into position, poised above the right spot, when a lock of the little boy's silky hair would obscure it again. And there were four to do altogether.

Dr Welland was first on call tonight, she knew, but it didn't seem worth calling him out for such a simple thing. On the other hand, Alex Evans was tired and miserable, and getting less easy to manage by the minute.

'I'll have to cut his hair,' Thea said. If Mr Evans was right in saying that the boy had been fretful all day, then these ticks had had a good chance to get well-embedded in the boy's skin. Revolting animals! she thought angrily.

'Yes, go ahead,' the boy's father said, so Thea got some scissors and began to snip away the hair above the nape of his neck and towards his right ear.

It had seemed like a simple problem ten minutes ago when the boy and his father first arrived, but now it was dark outside, the deputy director of nursing was at the far end of the building with a first-time mother in labour, and Thea, used to working in a hospital with over four hundred beds and even more staff, felt very alone.

Now that she had snipped away quite a bit of the boy's hair, she could see that the area around each tick was red and slightly swollen. She would need to put antiseptic on it afterwards and that would sting. Meanwhile, Alex was howling now, his face reddened and his cries approaching a toddler's uncontrollable hysteria.

I can't call Dr Welland now, Thea thought. It'll take several minutes for him to get here. . .

And then suddenly there was a sound in the open

doorway of the small examination-room and Joe was there. He wasn't dressed for work, but neither Thea nor Mark Evans noticed that.

'Looks as if we have a very unhappy little boy here,' Joe said cheerfully. 'Hey, little man, what's going on?'

He came into the room and picked up the child, undaunted by the fact that the screaming and writhing continued unabated. 'Ticks?' He looked up at parent and nurse.

'Yes, four of them,' Thea said, her competence returning just at the sight of Joe. 'I've cut his hair. They're quite deeply embedded.'

'Past his bedtime, isn't it?' Joe asked the twenty-month-old's father.

'Way past, and he didn't nap properly today either.'

'Look, I don't want you to feel concerned. . .' his low voice was calm and confident '. . .but I'm going to sedate him and keep him in overnight. These creatures can leave their nasty little heads behind if you're not careful, and with. . .what's his name?'

'Alex.'

'With Alex understandably in a state, I don't want to risk us not getting a proper look.'

'Sounds good to me,' the father said. 'Sorry, Nurse. He doesn't usually have tantrums like this, but. . .'

'Don't worry,' Thea said, not trusting herself with too many words. She felt a little shaky suddenly, and would have fallen in love with Joe Stockwell on the spot for his competent, friendly bedside manner. . .if she hadn't been in love with him already.

Joe filled a syringe with a dose of mild tranquilliser and quickly injected it into the plump cheek of the little boy's bottom. For several minutes, he screamed even louder in spite of his father's somewhat grim attempts to soothe him.

Then he quietened, his rosy little face relaxed, and

he made a miraculously swift transformation from hysteria to sleep.

'Lay him on his tummy over here on the examining table,' Joe said. 'And Sister, can you position the lamp a bit better? I really want to get a good look at this.'

He bent over the child with tweezers poised as Thea had vainly tried to do fifteen minutes ago. Now, with Alex sleeping, it was easy. Two of the ticks came out completely with the first pincer-like probe of the tweezers, but the third did leave its head behind and Joe had to get a sharp instrument to prise it out. The little boy stirred and made some fretful sounds but did not wake. The fourth tick, too, caused trouble but was eventually removed.

'That's it, I think,' Thea said, swooping in once more with swabs of antiseptic solution.

'Better do a thorough check,' Joe answered. His fingers were incredibly gentle as they probed painstakingly through the sleeping child's fine fair hair, and his effort was worthwhile. Another tick was found. 'It's a bad year for them, I've heard,' the doctor murmured as he picked up the tweezers once more. 'It's been so dry. Do you have a dog, Mr Evans?'

'Yes. We should have thought of that. . . We've rented a house a couple of blocks back from the beach and Alphabet goes haring off into the bush chasing goodness knows what.'

'Get a flea collar and some powder for him, and don't let him play with the kids while you're down here,' Joe suggested. 'You've got older ones as well?'

'Yes, twins, aged four and a half.'

'Check Alphabet for ticks and get as many off him as you can, and check the twins as well, including their clothing at the end of each day.'

'What a disaster!'

'No, it isn't,' Joe answered him seriously. 'The dog

is the main problem, and the fact that your house is backing directly on to the bush. Just stick to those glorious beaches and tidal lakes and rocky headlands.'

'Trouble is, the kids get sunburnt on the beach.'

'Got an umbrella?'

'Well, we've got one, but ——'

'Put it up. It's worth the trouble, and put hats and T-shirts on them, and sunblock cream. Aha!' He had been gently examining the little boy's body and clothing as he spoke, and now, tucked into a tender little crease of skin in the child's armpit, he had found yet another tick, which was soon deftly removed.

'You said you wanted to keep him in overnight. . .' The boy's father frowned.

'Yes, just to be extra-safe. We have the beds at the moment, so we might as well use them. He could develop a bit of fever after six ticks, each of them for several hours. I'll put him on a short course of anti-biotics as well, and I've got the little blighters to have a close look at tomorrow in my office.'

He held up the specimen jar in which the dead, bloated creatures were safely stored. 'Would you or your wife like to stay in here with Alex?'

'My wife would, I'm sure. She'll have got the twins to sleep by now. I'll drive back to the beach-house and she can have the car to come back here.'

'All settled, then,' Joe nodded cheerfully. 'Sister. . .?'

'Yes.' Thea quickly went to organise a bed for the little boy and found to her surprise that Judy Clinton had already arrived to take over. 'Is it ten o'clock already?' she exclaimed, after greeting the forty-five-year-old mother of three.

'Ten past,' Judy said. 'I gather you've had a bit of a drama.'

'Well, it might not have been,' Thea confessed, 'if I'd had more experience with ticks.'

'Ugh! Horrid things, aren't they? It's a really bad year for them.'

Thea settled the little boy in a bed for the night and then gathered her things ready to leave, telling Judy that Mrs Evans would soon be here to spend the night in the bed next to her child's. Sister Gleason, the deputy director of nursing, was busy again with the labouring expectant mother, who was now moving rapidly towards delivery.

Two more patients — an elderly man in for observation after a suspected mild stroke this morning, and a new mother, who had just returned her baby to the tiny nursery after its ten o'clock feed — were settling for the night in different rooms along the corridor. At the far end of the H-shaped hospital building, two ambulance officers whiled away their on-call time playing cards.

'A typical sort of night,' Judy Clinton told Thea.

The latter nodded, but if the truth were told her mind wasn't really on the light conversation she was having with Sister Clinton. She was actually wondering where Joe was. The wing of the building that led to Casualty, where little Alex had been examined and treated, was quiet now, and there was no sign of Dr Stockwell's tall figure in the front office. Had he just gone away again without saying anything? She was fairly certain that he had dropped in purely to see her. Was he angry at being roped in to treat those ghastly ticks when he wasn't even on call?

Thea wanted to say to Judy Clinton, Have you seen Joe? I thought he'd be waiting for me. . .but of course she couldn't, and the fact that she had to just say goodnight and leave the hospital reminded her too strongly of the pretence she was engaged in.

She *did* say goodnight, though, and hoped that Judy didn't notice her instinctive glance along the far corridor just before she turned down the corridor that led out to the front entrance. Still no sign of Joe.

Outside, the air had freshened after a hot dry day. Thea's shift had started at two but she had come in at half-past twelve, after an early lunch, wanting to get a head start on familiarising herself with the place. She had been nervous then, feeling somehow that she was on trial after her messy departure from Mount Royal Hospital, although she knew this was ridiculous. The feeling had stayed with her all day, although she had liked the hospital on sight, with its quiet, clean corridors and breezy position set back from the main highway at the top of a slope that gave views of the sea.

'Dr Carmichael's granddaughter, aren't you?' several people — both patients and doctors — had asked, and this brought home to her how widely her grandfather was known and respected in the community.

I mustn't let him down. She had known this before, of course, but it was an even stronger feeling now.

'Saw you at the wheel of Mrs Carmichael's car, behind the Conway Bay supermarket, on Saturday. Staying at the Carmichaels' place while they're away, are you?' another of the hospital's eight visiting general practitioners had asked.

'No, not at the moment,' Thea had said. 'They have some friends from England staying there for the first four weeks. I'm in a granny flat belonging to some *more* friends of theirs. But I'll be moving into their place at the end of four weeks, and, yes, I'm using my grandmother's car.'

Hester Carmichael's Citroën was a distinctive pink — the indulgence of a whim that the spirited former nurse was quite defiant and unrepentant about — and it was easy to pick out in this fairly small community of several linked coastal towns. It was parked now in a side-street, as the small hospital car park was reserved for doctors visiting or on call, but even here in the darkness its frivolous pink hue was noticeable.

I won't just be able to park it outside Joe's, Thea realised.

Still a little strung out after her unsuccessful grappling with the ticks, confused about what had happened to Joe, thinking about the wretched business of secrecy yet again, she was tired and tense as she reached the car and took out her keys. Their rattle and the opening of the car door masked the sound of commanding footsteps so that it wasn't until he was almost upon her that she saw Joe at last.

'Couldn't you wait?' he teased, dropping a kiss in her hair and winding arms around her.

'Not here!' she whispered fiercely, stiffening.

He drew back, his lips pressed tightly together. 'Why? Has Sister Gleason got her binoculars out?'

'No, but. . .' She felt petty now, but ploughed on anyway. 'People know this car. There are lights on in both those houses across the street. Anyone could——'

'I'd risk it for a kiss. . .' he answered, nuzzling his nose against hers, but Thea couldn't relax and he sensed the strain within her.

'Hey. . . Drive down to Wintooma Beach and I'll meet you there,' he said. 'We can go for a walk. It's a beautiful night.'

'What if——?'

'*No one* will see us!' She heard the edge of impatience in his tone.

'I'd love a walk on the beach,' she admitted.

'See you there, then.' He turned on his heel and went back up the street to the hospital car park.

How horrible this is, Thea thought. We can't even drive in the same car! I wonder if Charmaine and Ewan do that. . .travel separately to the same place?

Comparing herself and Joe with her former flat-mate and the detestable orthopaedic surgeon didn't help her to feel good about the situation. . .

Joe was already waiting for her in the small cleared space off the Princes Highway where beach-goers — most of them surf fishermen at this spot — parked their cars. He took her hand at once and they walked in silence across the spinifex-covered sandhill that dropped to a long, sloping stretch of beach.

Joe had been right. There was not a soul in sight. Breathing the tangy salt air, Thea felt tensions slipping away. The moon was waxing towards its half-full shape and gave enough light in the cloudless sky to make the sea shine with an almost phosphorescent blue-white. The waves lunged forwards and sank back with a rhythmic washing sound that had soothed human spirits down the ages.

'I can't walk on the beach in shoes,' Joe said abruptly, pulling his off and leaving them beside a post that marked the path they had come down.

'Neither can I.'

So they walked barefoot, feeling the sand at first silky and dry as it ran through their toes and then hard and wet and cold as they splashed along just where the waves teased the shore.

'I've never been to this beach before,' Thea said.

'Dangerous undertows, apparently,' Joe answered. 'People don't come here to swim, only to fish and walk, and since it's several miles out of town I thought it'd be safe. . .'

'Safe!' she echoed the word distastefully.

'Isn't that what you wanted?' he queried, betraying impatience.

'Not what I *wanted*! What we agreed on. What has to happen,' she said, her throat tightening. 'In fact, you suggested it.'

'I know.' He grimaced, and pulled her close suddenly. 'I thought it would be fun. . .in a way. . . But already it's not, is it?'

'No. . .'

'So you were right.' He coaxed her to stop and kissed her, his arms warm as they massaged her back, and his thighs hard against her own, until a bold wave splashed suddenly to their knees and made them break apart, laughing. Thea was feeling a lot better.

'Where did you go tonight?' she asked as they continued walking.

'You mean after little Alex was safely settled? I dropped in on old Mr King in Room Four. Dr Fane wants me to take him on as my patient.'

'I couldn't see you and I didn't dare look too hard. Thanks for stepping in with those ticks. I'd got in a little out of my depth.'

'It's bothering you, isn't it?'

'Yes. I should have seen earlier that Alex was going to get too hysterical, and I should have guessed that there might be more ticks than we'd already found.'

'Don't! For heaven's sake, it was your first day in a completely new situation.'

'Yours too.'

'Less of a challenge for me, I think. Internship and residency prepares you for far worse than that.'

'So does general nursing! I suppose I'm so concerned with seeming competent because I'm Dr Carmichael's granddaughter. I didn't want to call a doctor in. If you hadn't dropped in. . . Why *did* you drop in, anyway? Not just to see old Mr King?'

'Not to see Mr King at all. I would have left that until tomorrow morning if I hadn't wanted to see you.'

They walked and talked for another hour, turning back the way they had come when they reached the rocky headland that marked the northern end of the beach. Joe asked Thea how she had settled in and she told him about the granny flat tucked in under a substantial brick house up on Conway Head, and its neat little sitting-room whose windows gave her glimpses of the bay and the ocean, beyond stands of slim-trunked eucalpyts and tall coastal banksias.

Then she heard about his place, an old cottage on a side-street in Tooma itself, which he was already planning to buy and renovate if his work at the practice here was as satisfying as he hoped.

'You must see the cottage,' he told her.

'Yes, if ——'

'No, *don't* say it's too risky!' He rounded on her suddenly, stopping her in her tracks in the sand. 'We have to take *some* risks!'

'We can't,' she retorted, a harshness in her voice disguising the misery she felt. Every time the subject came up, it was horrible! 'I'm not prepared to. My grandfather was quite adamant about what he said, and he went out of his way to convince the hospital board that I'd be a good candidate for this job.'

'So you're saying that you're not going to come to my house if I ask you?'

'No, I'm not saying that. It's just. . . I'll have to leave my car at the hospital and walk over. Only come after dark, perhaps, and not come down Waratah Street, because Dr Bristow lives there.'

'And Sister Drummond lives in Porter Street so you can't come down that,' Joe put in. 'Which means you'll have to go all the way along to Coast Street, come down as far as Kingaman Road, turn down that for several hundred yards, and walk back up my street.'

'All right,' she agreed shortly. 'It's ridiculous, but from what I've seen of Sister Drummond. . .'

She trailed off and he didn't say anything. He wasn't touching her, either, at the moment. Ahead now she could see the place where they had left their shoes and where the path across the sandhill led back to those two lonely cars. Joe seemed to be increasing his stride as if he couldn't wait for this walk to be over.

Risking a sideways glance at him, she saw that he was frowning heavily, his mouth set in a straight, forbidding line. Quickening her pace, she still had trouble keeping up with him and when she allowed herself to slip back a little he made no comment and she wondered miserably if he had even noticed that she was no longer beside him.

Joe *hadn't* noticed. He was thinking intently and seriously, If I told her I loved her, asked her to marry me, would that make it better? No one could object then, could they? Dr Fane had told him about the drama involving Thea's predecessor at the hospital and a married visiting practitioner, Dr Peter Welland. It bore no similarity to his relationship with Thea, and he wondered if Thea herself knew the details.

No, he decided. It's too soon! *Far* too soon! I don't know what she feels. Perhaps for her this is just. . . who knows? As for me. . . No, I need more time as well. What if this *isn't* what I think it is? It'd be crazy and wrong to take a step like this because we're crumbling to outside pressures. It'd be a horrible way to have it happen. He could hear the exchange between them, practical, direct, sensible. *Not* how he wanted something like this to happen at all! My God, Joseph Stockwell! Are you a romantic at heart, then? Yes, I suppose I am. Is she? I wonder. You see, I don't know. And I *should* know. I think she is. That night at Mount Aspiring in the moonlight. . .

But already that seemed a long time ago, and his thoughts circulated back to their starting point once again: It was too soon. . .

He was still frowning and a little distant in his thoughts when he reached his car and turned to find Thea several yards behind him. 'Got your keys?' he asked her.

'Yes, I think so.'

'Better check. We both had better. Wouldn't it be crazy if one of us drove off and the other one was stuck here because of car trouble or a lost key?'

'Don't joke about it!'

They unlocked their car doors and Thea thought, He's not even going to kiss me. . .

But just as she was about to give up, wish him a neutral goodnight and climb in, he was beside her and she gasped as she felt him suddenly so close, so tall and warm. In another second she was a happy prisoner in his arms, reaching her hands hungrily around his neck to run her fingers through his thick but deliciously soft waves of hair.

His mouth sought hers with hot, unashamed impatience and she gave him her kiss, parting her lips to taste and explore him as tendrils of awareness formed a web of desire that stretched from the tips of tingling fingers to the most secret and sensitive places in her body. His hands moulded her slim hips then slid upwards till they found and cupped her tender young breasts, turning their delicate tips to points of fire.

There was a need in him tonight that she had not seen before, and although her own arousal and passion fully matched his she found that she was soon breathless and trembling, a little afraid of where this could go if she let him.

Does he realise how inexperienced I am? she wondered painfully. Will it make a difference to him? Should I tell him?

In the end, however, she said nothing, and he pulled away from her gently, making an effort to control the deep, ragged breaths that were pulling in and out of his strong chest. Brushing his nose one last time against hers and snatching a tiny, teasing kiss from her lips, he said, 'We should go. It's after midnight. Will you go first, and I'll follow?'

'Mmm-hmm,' she nodded, not yet trusting herself to speak properly.

Just the sight of him overwhelmed her sometimes, made her weak at the knees. Here in the darkness he was just a shape, a warm human sculpture, but the dim outline of his messed-up hair, strong shoulders and long thighs was enough to make her long for his support and his touch once again.

Not now. Too late at night. Too dangerous. With a careful, 'See you soon,' she got into the car, started it with fumbling fingers, and drove away.

# CHAPTER FIVE

'I'M WORRIED about Mr King,' Thea reported to Sister Drummond, the director of nursing, on Friday afternoon.

She had brought him a cup of tea twenty minutes earlier. It was a task that, in a big hospital like the one she was used to, would have been done by a member of the catering staff, but here, with only a handful of patients to care for, nurses brought tea or coffee, often at a patient's own request. That was the case with Mr King. He had asked for the hot drink when she had come in to make a routine check on his condition.

'Are you feeling all right, Mr King?' she had asked at the time, and he had said that he was.

He had made a good recovery from the initial stroke that had brought him into hospital, able to walk, dress and feed himself, and showing no difficulty with language after the first few days of mild aphasia. Now, though. . . She had gone in to take away his empty cup and although she had found it set neatly on the small chest of drawers by his bed Bert King himself had only looked at her with glazed eyes and had not responded to her greeting.

Sister Drummond frowned at Thea's report and murmured, 'Another stroke?'

'That's what I suspect. Still a mild one. He's conscious. Vital signs are good.'

'Let's see.' The rather formidable director of nursing led the way to the two-bed room at the male end of the corridor in which Mr King was currently the only patient.

Thea followed behind, wondering if her own generation of nurses would ever produce quite such commanding specimens as Joan Drummond. She had the classic silhouette of plump square shoulders, and rigid shelving bosom, and punctuated her immaculately clean uniform with the starched white cap that most hospitals had dispensed with now.

Thea had been told by the director of nursing that nurses at Tooma Community Hospital could wear caps of they wanted to, but it wasn't compulsory. Eyeing Sister Drummond's perfect arc, held in place by skilfully placed pins, Thea had politely said that she didn't think she would, thank you. She had no confidence that she would ever learn to keep it straight, though she didn't explain this qualm to Sister Drummond.

Ahead of Thea now, the white cap moved, beautifully symmetrical as usual. Joan Drummond had never married — by choice, rumour had it. She had just bought a beachfront house over at Narranook, the next beach south of Conway Bay, but hadn't yet moved from her cottage on Porter Street in Tooma itself. Nearing retiring age, she had begun to speak zestfully of what she would do at Narranook once she had left the hospital, but Thea knew that the transition would be a difficult one.

'Now, Mr King,' Sister Drummond began, entering the patient's room and with the sheer force of her personality calling a faint, confused response from him.

'Mmmh-mm. . .fell. In the shed. . .'

Sister Drummond bent over him, lifting his hands one at a time and studying his face. 'Yes,' she said after a minute, still studying the patient. 'Better phone Dr Fane.'

'Dr Stockwell,' Thea came in quickly and automatically.

'That's right,' the director of nursing nodded. 'Mr

King belongs to the new man now, doesn't he?' Her tone gave the distinct impression that she thought 'the new man' should find his own patients, although Joe had been taken on in the practice precisely because Dr Fane was overloaded.

'Then do you think it was another stroke?'

'It's certainly likely. Mr King, we were going to send you home tomorrow, dear!'

There was another inarticulate sound and then a crooked smile from the old man, so crooked that Thea said, 'Some hemiplegia? One side of his face isn't moving.'

'Looks like it.' Then in a low tone, 'We'll probably have to send him to Wollongong for a while. He may need the sort of care and therapy that's beyond us here, to regain speech and movement.'

'I'll phone Dr Stockwell.'

It wasn't the first time this week that Thea had had to do so, but she hadn't got used to it yet. Sister Drummond stayed with the patient, who was showing some signs of agitation and confusion now, as if he no longer knew where he was and why he was there. It was unfortunate. After that first mild stroke, and until then a healthy eighty-four, he had been doing so well, but now. . .

'Dr Stockwell?' Alone at the nurses' station, she hoped to hear his tone drop to a personal pitch that would tell her he was free to talk as well, but it didn't happen.

'Yes, Sister Carmichael?'

'Oh. . .' She couldn't help letting her voice fall a little in disappointment, then she realised, This is just what Grandpa didn't want to have — a nurse who would let personal feelings get in the way of her work. So she went on in a new, crisp voice, 'We think Mr King has had another stroke, a little more serious this time.'

'You want me there?'

'As soon as you can, yes. Sister Drummond thinks he may have to go to Wollongong.'

'I'm just about finished. I'm with a patient.' It was as Thea had guessed. 'Expect me in ten minutes.'

'Very good, Doctor.'

Sister Drummond was still in the patient's room when Thea ushered Joe in. It was obvious that the director of nursing thought 'the new man' absurdly young at twenty-nine. Even Dr Fane and Dr Welland, at forty-seven and forty-three, incurred her impatience and disapproval at times. Not about their modern medical methods — she was ruthlessly up-to-date in technical matters — but her protocol was proudly old-fashioned and would remain so, thank you very much!

Thea could not stay while Joe examined Mr King. A woman in her late thirties had just come in with her husband, clearly almost ready to give birth. 'It's my fifth so I know what I'm doing,' Mrs Milliken said comfortably, after breathing heavily through a strong contraction.

None the less, there were admitting procedures to be carried out and delivery-room equipment to be checked. Dr Lister, apparently, was already on his way.

A busy two hours followed. Mrs Milliken was, as she and her husband had suspected, almost fully dilated already, but the baby was large and she had some difficulty in pushing him out. Shaking her head at the suggestion of an episiotomy. . .'I've never needed one before!'. . .she unfortunately sustained quite a nasty tear that had to be stitched under local anaesthetic.

'The baby is beautiful,' Thea was able to tell her truthfully and the worst of the stitching was done while Mrs Milliken crooned to her little boy as he lay on her abdomen and Mr Milliken stroked his wife's hair.

Patients' dinner-hour had just ended when Thea was finally finished with the Millikens. Baby Robert was settled in the nursery while Mrs Milliken was resting in a room by herself. She had asked to have him 'rooming in' with her from tomorrow on — this hospital was small enough to be able to be very flexible about this sort of arrangement — but for tonight, all too experienced when it came to post-partum fatigue, Angela Milliken wanted some peace and quiet.

Elderly Dr Lister left, giving instructions for the night in his gruff manner on his way out. Thea collected empty dishes from the three patients who had eaten tonight. The hospital didn't have a kitchen for the preparation of meals. Instead the work was 'contracted out'. This was far simpler than it sounded. A capable woman living across the street from the hospital supplemented her husband's income by preparing meals for patients in her own kitchen and trundling them across in a covered trolley. When patients had finished eating, the dishes had to be collected and returned to the trolley, which Mrs Pyke returned for later in the evening.

There was no set of dishes for Mr King. 'Dr Stockwell agreed that Wollongong was the best place for him,' Sister Drummond informed Thea, phrasing it as if the doctor's decision had been a mere formality following her own judgement of the matter.

'Has he gone?' Thea couldn't help asking, hoping she'd get the chance for a private word with Joe. Their schedules hadn't dovetailed well this week. They had barely talked since Monday night.

'Yes, the ambulance took him an hour ago,' Sister Drummond said.

'The *ambulance*? Oh, yes, of course. Mr King. He would. . .' She trailed off, blushing and flustered. She had meant Joe, and of course Sister Drummond was talking about Mr King.

The director of nursing studied her closely for a moment, her jaw clamped shut and her bottom lip arching suspiciously. Thea didn't dare to ask again more specifically about Joe. He must have gone. He was on call tonight, but she didn't want to hope that he had to come in.

Why didn't we arrange on Monday night to see each other? she thought in frustration. Something definite. With our irregular hours. . . And again this secrecy! We can't just wait till chance throws us some time together. We have to make it happen! If he wants to. . . The doubt suggested itself, then she squashed it firmly. Nothing in Monday's final kiss had suggested he didn't want to see her again.

I'll just have to wait until he suggests something, she decided in the end, not very happily.

For the first time, and very briefly, she missed Charmaine. The older girl had provided racy advice in the past once, when Thea had had a short, unsatisfying yen for an anaesthetist she had barely even spoken to.

'Spill a cup of coffee all over him in the cafeteria. . . Or, better still, joggle his elbow so *he* spills it all over you!' the sophisticated redhead had advised coolly.

'*What*?'

'Well, isn't the idea for him to notice you? He'd notice you all right.'

No, thank you, Charmaine. The older nurse would have had no useful advice to offer about Joe.


'So much for sunset wading in tidal lagoons!' said a pretty blonde woman in her early thirties, stripping off makeshift bandages to show Thea several nasty cuts on her feet. Two of them were still bleeding quite heavily and she suspected that stitches might be needed. The woman spread a wide, mobile mouth in a grimace of pain and distaste.

'Oyster shells?' Thea asked quickly.

'Yes. That's why I came in here. I've heard that cuts from oyster shells can take a long time to heal.'

'Yes, and they're very prone to infection as well,' Thea said. 'You were wise to come in.'

Quickly, she went to ring the on-call doctor — Joe again. It was Saturday night. Returning to the new patient, Thea took another look at the cuts. There were three on one foot and two on the other. All of them needed cleaning as each contained sand and shell grit. It was difficult work, and Thea knew it must be painful for the patient. What was her name? It was written here on this patient information sheet. Jessica Lewis.

'Are you here for a holiday?' Thea asked.

'No, I live in Shellhaven.' She named the moderate-sized town only three miles away that had once been a tiny fishing port but had now, through tourism and retiree settlement, grown to eclipse the older Tooma and encroach upon the beach villages of Conway Bay and Narranook. 'I own the health-food shop there.'

'Oh! I was in there the other day to pick up some provisions. You have a really good range. But it wasn't you who——'

'No, my assistant, probably.' Jessica Lewis winced. Thea had had to resort to tweezers to remove a particularly stubborn piece of grit.

'I'm sorry about this,' the nurse said, 'but if I don't get it all out. . .'

'I know. It'll get infected. Go ahead. Are you nearly finished?'

'Yes. But as we were saying. . .' Thea knew that conversation was a sure distraction to pain. 'Yes, it must have been your assistant. An older woman.'

'Maggie. Maggie Blaines. She and her husband had retired down here, then he died only a few months afterwards. She doesn't need the money, but she loves to have something to do and people to chat to.'

'Yes, she certainly likes to chat!'

'I'm sorry. She can be a bit slow. . .'

'Don't worry. I enjoyed it.'

'Is this a private foot bath, or can anyone join in?' Joe Stockwell said, appearing in the open doorway just as Thea decided she had finally cleaned the cuts thoroughly.

He gave a very quick, private glance to Thea, who returned it with a special smile that had to be cut off quickly when Jessica said, 'Hello, Joe! I was wondering if it would be you!'

'Well, I never!' the doctor exclaimed as he washed his hands carefully. 'Jessica, isn't it? I won't say, "Nice to see you again", because I'm sure you wish you *weren't* here with those feet.'

'Oh. . .' She shrugged with a smile, as if the oyster-shell lacerations had suddenly reaped an unexpected benefit. 'How was that herbal tea I recommended?'

'Delicious, thanks. Very light and refreshing for summer, just what I wanted.'

They went on talking while Joe examined the cuts, referring several times to the conversation they had evidently had in Jessica Lewis's health-food shop the other day. Her assistant isn't the only one who likes to talk to customers, it seems, Thea decided.

She struggled against the feeling but couldn't help a tinge of. . .not jealousy, surely? That was too strong a word. But it was so. . .upsetting that this woman, who had met Joe only once, apparently, could chat to him so freely while she herself had to be circumspect, almost terse.

He was talking to her in the same way. 'Sister, you

were right,' he said now, without so much as a glance in her direction. 'These two on the left foot do need a stitch each. I'll do them now, then I'll leave you to dress these other shallower ones.'

'Of course,' she murmured.

They worked quickly together over the process of suturing the two jagged cuts under local anaesthetic. It wasn't a difficult job, although one cut, slicing between Jessica Lewis's second and third toes, was in an awkward position. Thea had each piece of equipment ready just when Joe needed it, the procedure was soon completed, and he flung a brief, 'Thanks!' at her before tossing filmy disposable gloves into a waste-bin and preparing to leave the room.

He's just going to leave, Thea realised. And of course it would be unnatural for him to do anything else. 'Bye, Doctor', she managed through a tightened throat, but then she noticed that he was hanging back by the door.

He cleared his throat. 'Keep yourself off those for a day or two, Jessica, if you can.'

'I'll see if Maggie can put in some extra hours in the shop.'

'Do that. Er—nice surprise to have a patient that I already knew personally. . .'

'Oh, yes! Lovely for me, too.' Jessica dimpled, her eyes shining. 'Actually,' she went on smoothly, 'I'm looking for a new general practitioner. Did you say you're in practice with Dr Fane now?'

'Yes.'

'Permanently?'

'I. . .hope so.'

'Should I make an appointment with you next week some time, then, to see if these are healing?'

'Yes, you'd better. Those stitches aren't the ones that dissolve. I'll need to take them out.'

'I'll look forward to it. . . To seeing you, that is, not having the stitches out.' There was a catlike purr in her tone, then a husky laugh.

'So will I,' Joe drawled.

Thea, her back turned as she worked on dressing Jessica's three more minor cuts, disliked Joe's tone. He didn't normally sound like that—flirty, superficial, deliberately sexy. No, she didn't like it at all!

'Goodnight, Sister,' he added, this time in a tone that was crisp and quite without emotion.

When he had safely gone, Jessica ran a hand through her wild mane of frosted curls and said throatily, 'Gosh! He's a bit of a charmer, isn't he?'

'I've only met him a few times,' Thea prevaricated, hating the lie.

'So have I. Twice, including tonight! Most doctors, though. . . I find them too clean, too urbane, as if they pickle themselves in antiseptic every night.'

'Ugh!'

'Exactly! But he's different. . .don't you think?'

'I suppose so.' Thank goodness she had almost finished the last cut!

'There's something earthy about him,' Jessica Lewis mused languorously. 'Natural and rugged. Since I'm into natural health, I like that in a man. Do you know if he's *attached*?'

She might as well have said 'fettered', and asked the question confidently, her brown eyes meeting Thea's grey-green ones unblinkingly. They weren't a dark brown, those eyes, but tawny with golden lights. Tiger's eyes. . . She evidently enjoyed taking on the role of predator, and didn't mind if other people saw her doing it.

'I. . . I think he *is* attached. I'm not sure,' Thea said in a slightly strangled tone. This time, it was a completely truthful reply.

'Hmm.' Jessica narrowed her eyes now, till only a golden glint showed between long, luxurious lashes. '*Not sure*, eh? Because *he's* not sure, or because you've just heard rumours? What is it? An old flame in Sydney? Didn't he used to live there?'

'Please,' Thea blurted, betraying too much emotion. 'I really don't know. This is. . . We're not supposed to get too personal with other members of staff. You're putting me in a difficult position.'

'Sorry.' Jessica Lewis bit her lip. The tiger had suddenly become a chastened kitten. 'I guess after that weird business of Dr Welland and poor Sister Thirkell the hospital is a bit sensitive about that sort of thing.'

'Yes, that's right,' Thea said. She still hadn't heard the story. . .still didn't want to, really. . .but evidently everyone else in the community knew it, or thought they did.

'I understand, then. I won't say anything more.'

'Anyway,' Thea came in quickly, 'I've finished now. Take the dressings off those three smaller cuts in a day or two, and put Band-Aids on them if they still look too raw. Do you have antiseptic powder at home?'

'No, I don't think so. Do I need a prescription for it? Perhaps Dr Stockwell——'

'You don't need a prescription,' Thea interrupted her firmly. 'Just go to the chemist and ask. There are several brands. Antiseptic cream, too, which you might prefer. It's up to you.'

'Thanks for your help.' The owner of the health-food shop spoke brightly, but Thea could tell she felt a little rebuffed and rebuked on the issue of Dr Stockwell. It couldn't be helped.

I don't want to be her confidante, Thea decided. If she's going to try and pursue Joe, I don't want to be involved. If only she could make it clearer to the woman that Joe was 'not available'. But it was impossible.

Dr Stockwell would have to do that himself. Assuming that he saw the situation in the same way. . .

'Thea?'

'Yes?' It was Joe, at ten o'clock on Sunday morning, and suddenly Thea's heart was light.

'Thank goodness we've connected at last! With you on a nine days on, four days off rotation and me with office hours and the on-call roster. . .'

'I was beginning to think we'd never coincide,' she finished for him.

'Yes! Can we coincide today?' His voice dropped to its low, caressing pitch, and she wanted to laugh with happiness.

'I start work at two, though.' It was a sobering reminder to herself and to him.

'Brunch, then,' he suggested cheerfully after a moment. 'Did you sleep in? Have you had breakfast?'

'Yes. . .and no, in that order,' she answered. In fact, she was still in her nightgown.

Last night's shift had finished at ten, and it always took her an hour or two to unwind after work. Having got to sleep late, she had lain in bed late this morning. Now, all at once, with the silky folds of her mauve summer nightdress still whispering around her skin and a light breeze moving the trees she could see outside against a blue sky as she talked on the phone, she was impatient for the day to begin.

'Will you come round, then?' Joe was saying.

'I'd love to.'

'Half an hour?'

Thea hurried to shower and dress, choosing a cinnamon-brown sleeveless blouse polka-dotted in white, and teaming it with its matching above-the-knee divided skirt. She drove to Joe's in her grandmother's pink car and parked it down on Kingaman Road beside the showground, where it was just conceivable that a passer-by who recognised the vehicle would think she had gone for an exploratory walk.

The day was glorious. It was March now, but the afternoons were still frequently hot enough for swimming and on a day like today when the sky was so brilliantly blue that it looked as if it had been freshly lacquered the sea air invited thoughts of ocean bathing.

Do we dare, if there's time? Thea wondered. I love the way he swims, like a playful horse. . .

The smell of fresh seafood greeted Thea's nostrils as Joe opened the door for her. 'Too early for you?' he asked anxiously as he pulled her into his kitchen. 'It's not a traditional brunch menu.'

'No! I'm starving!'

'There's fresh fruit salad to start,' he promised, sitting her down at a wooden kitchen table dressed up with a cheery seersucker cloth.

'Can't I help?'

'No, it's almost done. I'm just squeezing some juice. Do you want coffee? Tea?'

'Not with seafood.'

'Wise decision.'

She watched happily as he worked, his strong hands twisting orange halves on a green glass orange-squeezer. For a while they were silent, then he looked up with a grin to say, 'So. . .like my place?'

'I haven't actually seen it. Shall I look?'

'If you like. It's a mess.' He added hastily, 'I don't mean clothes all over the floor, but you'll see.'

She went to explore. This enclosed veranda with its light, airy feeling was delightful, for a start, although the kitchen fittings were old-fashioned and the linoleum on the floor in there was worn. Here on the veranda there was seagrass matting and bright prints on the walls, a squishy couch covered in cushions and several potted plants. The sitting-room and two small bed-rooms *were* 'a mess', as he had said, mainly due to the previous resident's unfortunate taste in wallpaper and carpets.

'The sale should go through in a couple of months,' he said, unable to resist following her to glean her response. 'Meanwhile, I'm getting a head start, as you can see.'

'You've done a lot already.'

'Time on my hands in the evenings, sometimes, when I'm not on call. You've been working,' he accused, accompanying the words with a caress on her shoulder that made Thea begin to tingle.

'My next rotation is mornings,' she said.

'Good!'

Thea wandered around the smaller front bedroom that he had started to strip. Layers of old wallpaper lay in curls and tears on the floor, revealing patches of previous paintwork, some an attractive cream, others a ghastly hot pink. 'The cream would suit this room,' she murmured.

'Yes, I'm planning to——'

He broke off. Footsteps had sounded on the wooden veranda at the front and now there was a loud knock at the door. Peering through the dingy double layer of old lace curtains he had not yet had a chance to replace, Joe said in an odd tone, 'It's Jessica Lewis.'

'Oh.'

'Duck into the back bedroom. If we're quiet, she might go.'

They crept into the other bedroom — his bedroom — and waited. But a minute later he said under his breath, 'Damn! What's she doing? Going round the side to see if my car's in the driveway. And of course it is. I'll have to let her in.'

Without another word he closed the door on Thea, leaving her alone in the dark bedroom. It wouldn't be dark when Joe had finished with it. She knew he wanted to enlarge the southern window and add a glass French door to open on to an extension of the veranda. Seeing it in her imagination, she knew that the cottage would be a dear little place when it was all done, with a bright cottage garden all around it. The perfect first home for a young couple, in fact. Just now, though, this boxy bedroom with its glaring felt wallpaper in purple, mustard and black wasn't where she wanted to be.

'Hi!' Thea heard Jessica Lewis's chirpy yet at the same time seductively throaty voice coming from the region of the front door. Then footsteps told her that Joe had ushered her — reluctantly? — into the house. 'I really just came to bring this.' There was the crackle of paper. Evidently a leaflet of some kind.

'Hmm, looks interesting,' came Joe's deep voice.

'It will be. It's a workshop on alternative healing. I'm bringing down a *wonderful* man from Sydney for it in about two months' time. He's really incredible, and I thought as a health professional you might want to explore some of these alternative options to healing.'

'I'll take a look at it.'

'Mmm, wow!' Jessica breathed now. 'What have you got cooking?'

'Just seafood. I'm having people to brunch.'

'It smells fabulous!'

'I'd love to ask you to stay, but —' His voice dropped to the throaty drawl that Thea hated.

'No, no,' Jessica came in quickly, taking the hint. 'I can't stay. I'm run off my feet this morning. I just really, really wanted you to have this.'

She made the leaflet about the workshop sound like a rare seashell or a beloved personal memento.

'I'm *so* glad you thought of me,' Joe said. They were stepping towards the front door and on to the veranda.

'Well, of *course* I thought of you!' It was kittenish and syrupy.

'See you round. . .'

The door had closed, thank goodness. There followed a silence that was stretching Thea's nerves to snapping point when suddenly she heard Joe's footsteps and the bedroom door opened at last.

'Wanted to wait till she drove away,' he explained. 'Did you feel like a prisoner in there?'

'Yes.'

'Sorry. . .' He pulled her into his arms and buried his face in her hair so that she could feel the fanning of his warm breath. Then he kissed her slowly and sweetly until she forgot all about Jessica Lewis.

She remembered later, though, as she and Joe ate fresh, crusty wholemeal bread, succulent prawns, sea-tanged oysters and sweet-fleshed fish, all just hours from the ocean. Squeezing lemon on to her oysters, she wondered, Shall I mention Jessica? I want to. Laugh about it with him. . . And maybe ask in a teasing sort of way if he would have asked the other woman in for coffee had he been alone.

Twice she took in breath ready to voice the subject and twice she said nothing and reached for another morsel of fish instead. Joe didn't mention the health-food shop owner, either.

'When did the pains start?' Thea asked the anxious woman who lay on her left side in one of the small hospital's two-bed rooms. Carefully, she placed pillows under the new patient's legs, elevating them slightly.

'An hour ago. . .wasn't it, Chris?' the patient asked her husband.

'Bit more than that, love. By the time we got your mother round to mind the kids. . .'

Mrs Watterson was just over three months pregnant, and the contractions she was experiencing were an alarming development. Pre-term labour at this stage, if it could not be stopped, would result in the loss of the baby.

'How often were they coming, the contractions?' Thea asked now.

'About every ten minutes.'

'Fairly regularly?'

'Yes. Trying to get the kids to bed, though. . . It was a while before it really clicked what was happening. They're not too painful,' she added hopefully. 'Maybe it's nothing.'

'The doctor will be here soon,' Thea soothed. 'He'll decide what's going on.'

She had phoned Joe, although he was not the doctor on call tonight, because Glenda Watterson was his patient and he had mentioned to Thea the other day that he was worried about her.

'I'd like to send her to Dr Hill,' he had said.

'The obstetrician in Wannego?'

'Yes. She's forty-one, with two other young children. She's a fair bit overweight. I'd consider her at higher than normal risk in any case, and she's big for her dates as well. I'm starting to wonder if there's more than one baby in there.'

This episode—Thea hoped it would turn out to be only an episode—of pre-term labour seemed to add grounds to Joe's concern. He was pleased that Thea had rung him, and entered the ward a few minutes later, slightly out of breath as if he had run all the way from the car park.

Immediately he began firing questions at Mrs Watterson, with a mixture of briskness and patience that made him both an effective doctor and a comforting one. 'Any cramping?'

'Yes, you mean. . . I had some diarrhoea just before I came in.'

'Discharge?'

'I hadn't noticed.'

Soon he established that the danger of pre-term labour continuing was real and began a course of intravenous ritodrine, one of a group of drugs called beta-mimetics, which relaxed the uterine muscles and slowed contractions.

'Mrs Watterson, at your office visit the other day. . .' Thea, still helping the patient to settle in and recording details on the chart at the foot of the bed, heard the reluctance in Joe's tone '. . . we discussed the question of your going to Dr Hill for your prenatal care.'

'Yes, and I told you I didn't want to,' the patient answered shortly.

'It's impossible, Doctor,' her husband put in placatingly. He was in his mid-forties and was slightly overweight as well. 'For one thing, he's fifteen miles up the coast. She doesn't drive, and with the other kids to look after. . .'

'And for another, I don't like him!' Glenda Watterson added. 'I went to him for an ultrasound when I was pregnant with Todd. I thought he seemed very cold.'

'Yes. . .' Joe said, frowning. 'I know he can seem that way. You're not the only person who has said that to me. . .'

'I like you. You seem good.'

'. . . but medically he's excellent.'

'I don't care about medically. Aren't you good medically? You're telling me you don't know what you're doing when you deliver a baby?'

'Of course I know what I'm doing, Mrs Watterson, but there's more to it than that.'

Thea could see that Joe was having trouble with this. She had met Mrs Watterson's type before. Such patients didn't necessarily have bad intentions, but they did have very strong goals and didn't hesitate to try and manipulate medical staff to try and get their way. In this case, Mrs Watterson's goal was to stay under Dr Stockwell's care. Very flattering for him, but it was putting her welfare and the safety of her pregnancy at risk.

'I don't have the equipment, Mrs Watterson — an ultrasound scanning machine, for example — and I *don't* have the experience with the complications that can occur in a multiple birth.'

'What do you mean, multiple birth?' Chris Watterson came in suspiciously.

But Glenda Watterson only said on a sigh, 'You mean it *is* twins. I've been wondering. I've felt *so* big and sick and tired, far worse than I did with Michelle and Todd.'

'Yes,' nodded Joe. 'You're very large for your dates, and this pre-term labour you're experiencing is another potential indicator. So *please* will you allow me to send you to Dr Hill for an ultrasound, then we'll make our decisions from there?'

'Not now?' The patient narrowed her eyes.

'No. When we've got this labour under control. I'll keep you in here for a couple of nights, and ——'

'Keep me *in*? How can I stay here? Michelle and Todd ——'

'Your mum'll just have to stay, love,' Chris came in.

'No! You know how she gets with them after a while. . . Doctor, just give me whatever it is I have to take, and ——'

'Mrs Watterson, you're staying in hospital.' This

time, bedside manner or no bedside manner, there was something so decisive in Dr Stockwell's tone that both the Wattersons were meekly silent.

Ten minutes later, unasked, Thea brought a cup of tea to the small consulting-room near the casualty entrance where Joe sat.

'Thanks!' he said.

'Thought you might need it.'

'I didn't want to tell her it could be triplets. The H.C.G. level in the blood test I did on her first visit was pretty high. Her dates could be wrong, but she seemed very sure about them.'

'If it *is* triplets, then she'll have to agree to see Dr Hill.'

'No!' He gave a hollow laugh and rubbed his eyes, after putting down the teacup that was already half drained. 'If it's triplets I'll want to send her to Sydney from about six months on. . .and possibly sooner if there are any more episodes of this pre-term labour.'

He sat in gloomy silence for a minute while Thea studied him sympathetically. He looked so thoroughly male, flung out in a swivel chair with his long legs stretching in front of him, yet at the same time, at this moment, so heart-stoppingly vulnerable. His hair was a mess and she itched to take out a comb and tidy those brown locks, although she loved the way they fell over his high forehead. Not that she'd dare to do such an intimate thing here at the hospital, of all places. . .

Then, just as she was thinking this, two long arms snaked out and caught her around the waist, pulling her back towards the chair and into his lap so that he could kiss her and possessively caress the rounded curves that were accentuated when she sat.

'We mustn't,' she whispered against his mouth, but he gave a low laugh and ignored her completely.

A knock—it sounded to Thea as startling as gunfire—came at the door and they sprang apart. Her breathing came in shallow gasps. Several minutes had passed. Her hair was a mess. Thank goodness she *hadn't* decided to wear a cap! His shirt was open an extra button at the neck. Her uniform was twisted, *and* she was blushing. She could feel the colour and heat creeping up her neck, and she knew that she always blushed so fiercely.

'Come in!' Joe had to clear his throat before he could speak.

The door opened to reveal Sister Drummond's impressive silhouette, just as Thea's colour reached its height. The director of nursing's knife-sharp eyes took in the guilty tableau. Joe had pulled open a file drawer. Thea had crazily seized a telephone directory. Sister Drummond said nothing for a moment. Perhaps the scene *did* look innocent after all. Then, very crisply, 'There's an English couple just come in. I couldn't find you at first, Sister. Or you, Doctor. I thought you'd gone. The wife seems very upset. I think you should see her at once.'

'Of course.' He cleared his throat again. 'Sister—um—er—Sister and I were just. . .'

'They're waiting in the examination-room next door.'

'Very good. Thank you, Sister.'

'Do I need to remind you that there is rarely an appropriate time for personal conversation at this hospital, Doctor? Nurse?'

'No, of course you don't, Sister,' Joe said, speaking for them both. Thea could only mutter a meaningless syllable.

'I didn't think so. . . By the way, Mrs Watterson says her contractions seem to be easing.'

'Yes. The ritodrine. . .' But the director of nursing had gone.

Joe's temples were misted in sweat. 'I couldn't

remember your name,' he said to Thea through a tight throat.

'What?'

'Didn't you hear? I couldn't remember it. Carmichael *Carmichael*. You see, I only ever think of you as Thea.'

'I don't think she noticed.'

'That's not the point.' He was angry now.

'No, I know,' she agreed in a low voice.

'We're letting this get to us in all sorts of ways, and we mustn't.'

'I know.'

'We're both making important early impressions in these jobs. We can't afford to think of each other as —— '

'I *know*, Joe!'

Still frowning heavily, he swore softly under his breath, the words hissing between clenched teeth. They left the consulting-room in silence, entered the examination-room next door and greeted the English couple rather tersely, their tension still betraying itself in tight shoulders and tighter faces.

The couple were elderly, each with white hair, and were dressed for a walk on the beach on a warm evening. The woman was crying and clutching her legs, chafing at them, and clearly in considerable pain and distress. Her husband, deeply anxious, was trying to remain calm.

'My wife has been stung by several jellyfish,' he explained at once. 'I'm told they're not dangerous. . . Small creatures with a blue, air-filled membrane and long trailing blue stingers.'

'Bluebottles,' Joe said briefly. He had bent down to examine the irregular rows of blotchy marks on the trembling legs. 'No, they're not dangerous. Painful, though.' He touched the distressed patient on the shoulder with an absent pat. 'Especially when you're not expecting it.'

'Please do something,' the man said, clearly very upset at the thought of his wife in pain.

'I'm going to leave it to Sister Carmichael.' Joe said Thea's name so firmly that it came out like a harsh bark. 'Don't worry. As I said, it's nothing serious. Nasty shock. Sister Carmichael will give you something for the pain.'

On these words, he left the room abruptly.

'Which is Sister Carmichael?' the Englishman asked, bewildered.

'Me,' Thea answered, aware that Joe hadn't looked at her at all as he spoke.

'Oh. Very well. . .'

Thea went to a cupboard and took out a remedy that most of the locals used on bluebottle stings. She wasn't sure of its chemical properties and it certainly wasn't listed in any pharmaceutical register, but it seemed to work and the hospital always kept a bottle of it on hand. Every summer they had several people come in with stings, usually tourists, apparently. Locals knew that the stings weren't serious and that they disappeared more quickly than a bee or wasp sting. She also took out a couple of mild pain-killers and gave them to the still trembling woman, along with a glass of water.

'I thought our holiday here was going to be so idyllic,' the patient said now that she was calmer. 'James and Hester painted such a glowing description, and now——'

'Come along, Miriam,' her husband said. 'It *is* idyllic, isn't it? Apart from this rotten piece of luck.'

'Luck? If the beaches are always awash with those horrible creatures. . .'

'They're not,' Thea promised.

She knew now who the English couple were—the

friends of her grandparents who were staying in their
house — and felt doubly unhappy, not just about the
stings but about the way she and Joe had been so
awkward and he, in particular, so blunt. It *won't*
happen again! she told herself. Then, aloud, 'You just
have to know when to watch out for bluebottles. It's
almost always when we have a north-easterly wind. It
blows them in, you see, in fleets. Those blue bubbles
of theirs act like sails. Locals take a look at the beach
and if they see a clutch of them freshly washed up they
don't go swimming that day. Fortunately, they're easy
to spot once you know.'

'I thought that blue colour was so pretty at first,' said
Mrs Abernethy. . . Thea had remembered the couple's
name now. 'I stopped to look, and a wave washed up
to my knees and wrapped those horrid trailing stings
around me.'

'Please.' Thea touched her gently. 'It's over now,
and it won't happen again. Is this funny stuff doing any
good?' She was swabbing the brown liquid on the stings
as she spoke.

'Yes, actually, I think it is.' Mrs Abernethy began to
brighten further.

'And now. . . I think you know my grandparents. . .'
Thea began, and explained who she was.

After they understood, the Abernethys were very
pleased to meet Thea, inviting her to dinner the
following week, and since all was quiet at the hospital
now she was able to seat them comnfortably in the
empty patients' sitting-room, bring them cups of tea
and stay to chat. 'We should have known your name
when that doctor said it,' John Abernethy said. 'But
we were so upset, it didn't click.'

'And with the man's awful manner!' Mrs Abernethy
came in, speaking in a confiding tone. 'My poor dear,
is he an ogre to work for?'

'No, he's not,' Thea said, suppressing a sigh. 'He's not, actually.' Then, the sort of white lie that she suspected she would have to get used to. . . 'I don't know what was the matter with him tonight.'

# CHAPTER SIX

'BY CRIKEY, I needed this!' Joe Stockwell said to Thea Carmichael as they thumped comfortably along the flat middle section of the walking track that led to the distinctively shaped summit of Pigeonhouse Mountain.

Boronia and wattle bordered the track, which at first had been steep and rough, and ahead beckoned the rocky summit. To the left, the jagged-edged escarpments of the Budawang Ranges were washed in layer upon layer of different blues, and, to the right, forests of eucalyptus gave way to farmlands and glimpses of distant, hazy ocean.

It was a glorious afternoon, and the first they had been able to spend together in the two weeks since each started work in the region. Thea had almost cried with relief three nights ago when Joe had phoned to suggest the expedition. He avoided her at the hospital now, calling for another nurse's help whenever he could, or speaking with his back to her, issuing brief, terse orders which she always hurried to obey without wasting words in chat.

She knew *why* he was so terse and distant, of course. He was too afraid — not only of betraying their secret but of being distracted from his work and perhaps missing some critical sign or symptom.

He hates the secrecy as much as I do, she thought.

But his way of dealing with it was different. She hoped, often, that he would ring her at home to talk, even if it could only be a snatched, five-minute call, but he didn't, and she didn't dare to ask why. Did he just hate the phone, or. . .? Perhaps the fact that they couldn't be open about seeing each other was putting him off. . .*cooling* him off.

So when his phone call *did* come, she accepted his suggestion eagerly—perhaps too eagerly—and swallowed a desire to thrash things out. Perhaps he would feel that there wasn't anything to say. . .

And now it seemed that her doubts were all foolish. He seemed relaxed, happy to be with her, keen to recapture the carefree mood they had had together in New Zealand. He was walking ahead of her now, carrying the small day-pack that contained chilled fruit juice, nuts, and some chewy oatmeal and coconut biscuits to snack on once they reached the top. The pack bounced lightly on his strong shoulders and he hadn't even worked up a sweat, still ridiculously fit and well toned after his long, active holiday in New Zealand.

'I needed this too,' she confessed to him, and he reached out and took her hand to pull her alongside him, although there was barely room for the two of them to walk abreast on this path.

Thea felt fabulous to Joe, against his arm. Small yet strong, warm, eager, with the same love of outdoor things as he had, and the same contentment about not talking unless there was something to say.

It's right, he thought. It *is* right. I'm sure of it. Shall I say it now, then perhaps it'll be easier when we see each other at the hospital?

He hesitated, still afraid that he would be rushing her, that he had been reading too much into the heat of her lips when she moved them so delightfully against his. Hang it, *surely* he wasn't reading her wrongly! Impulsively, he opened his mouth to say the words that he hoped would seal things between them, but. . .

'Are you going to that workshop Jessica Lewis is running?'

'What?' For a moment, he didn't even know what she was talking about, and the brief question came out more abruptly than he had intended. Then he remembered. Jessica Lewis, the owner of the health food shop. An attractive woman in some ways, but not really his type. . .especially not now. 'Oh, her!' he said dismissively, wishing Thea hadn't chosen just *this* moment to mention the woman and her workshop. At any other time he could have laughed about it with her, but now, his first impulsive certainty ebbing and feeling surprisingly nervous as he wondered how to say to Thea. . .

'Yes, her,' she was saying impudently. 'Haven't you noticed that you've got her in the palm of your hand?'

'Oh, I've noticed.'

To Thea the words sounded abrupt, cool, and she was sorry she had brought up the subject. Why did I? she wondered. The answer wasn't hard to find. I suppose I'm a little threatened by her.

It seemed ridiculous to feel this way, when Joe's arm was still so delightfully heavy and strong around her shoulders, but she couldn't help it. Perhaps it was because Jessica reminded her of Charmaine. Not in looks. The willowy, amost too-thin redhead and the petite, well-rounded blonde could scarcely have been more dissimilar physically. But both women had an aggressive, over-confident quality that Thea lacked, and although she didn't particularly admire the quality she had seen that in Charmaine's case it had won her the man she desired.

Jessica Lewis clearly desired Joe Stockewll. . . I'm being an idiot! Thea scolded herself. She put the subject out of her mind and tried to regain the contented mood she had been sharing with Joe five minutes earlier. Something was missing, though. He seemed preoccupied, dissatisfied. He wasn't still thinking about Jessica, was he?

Then she saw a movement in the bushes to the left of the path and stopped, holding Joe back. 'Shh! That's not a snake, is it?'

'Where?'

'Oh the other side of that rock. I saw a movement and the flick of a long tail.'

'Not a snake, I don't think.' He was following her gesture and peering into the bush. 'No, it's a goanna.'

'Really! Yes, so it is.'

They both studied the silent creature for several seconds, barely breathing. He was a small fellow by goanna standards, only two or three feet long, well camouflaged against the lichen-encrusted rocks. Sitting up on his front legs ready to make a dash for it, the lizard studied them with unwinking eyes, then suddenly he was gone, incredibly nimble on those knotty, clawed limbs.

'Scared?' Joe asked, holding her more tightly.

'No. . .' But she laid her head down on the muscular breadth of his shoulder all the same. 'They can be a little startling, though, can't they, if you're not expecting that quick movement?'

'Yes. Old bush lore says they keep snakes at bay, but I've never known whether to believe it.'

'Let's believe it for today. We don't want to spoil our walk by expecting a snake on the far side of every rock!'

He laughed and things felt good again. They reached the top, breathing heavily on the steeper section towards the end and then tackling several long metal ladders bolted into the near-vertical faces of the plug-shaped summit. At the top, the view was magnificent, offering glimpses into rainforest-filled gullies that looked so inaccessible they might never have known a human tread. In those gullies there would be cool, gurgling creeks, the lush green fronds of tree ferns and secretive lyrebirds with their incredible range of mimicking calls.

Up here, it was hotter and drier, but they found some dappled shade and sat on the rocks, slaking their thirst with icy juice and replenishing energy with nuts and biscuits. They didn't hurry to leave the summit. One or two groups of people came and went, signing their names in the visitors' book and commenting on the view, but they didn't intrude on Thea and Joe's contentment together.

Then an elderly couple appeared, taking the last winding yards on rocks and narrow path slowly and with care. Thea was lazily admiring their sturdy hiking get-up—strong walking shoes, thick protective knee socks, roomy khaki shorts and smart buttoned cotton shirts, each in a different plaid pattern—when she suddenly realised that she knew them. In fact, she had been to dinner at a restaurant with them three days ago. It was Mr and Mrs Abernethy.

Instinctively, she began to scramble to her feet, seeking a hiding place, but Joe quietly put out an arm to restrain her, saying, 'Too late. They've seen us. Better to act naturally. They won't think to mention it to anyone, surely.'

Act naturally! Thea found it hard. The couple approached and greeted doctor and nurse cheerfully. 'Magnificent, isn't it?'

'Yes, and such a perfect day, too,' Thea agreed. She had enjoyed her meal with the Abernethys, but found it difficult to be as relaxed with them now as she had been the other night.

'Your grandparents told us we mustn't miss this climb, and they were right,' Mr Abernethy said.

'Bluebottle stings all healed?' Joe asked the Englishman's wife with a smile.

'Oh, yes! By the next day they were barely noticeable, thank you.' Mrs Abernethy's manner was a little reserved as she remembered how abrupt the doctor had seemed that day in the hospital.

'Is this your first time up here?' Mr Abernethy put in quickly, evidently willing to forget their first impression of Dr Stockwell.

'Yes,' Joe nodded, then added easily, 'We discovered by chance that we both wanted to do the climb, and decided we might as well do it together.'

'So you're both new to the area?'

'Yes.'

'Well, you picked a good place to live,' Mr Abernethy said firmly. 'I admit that the bluebottle jellyfish experience didn't give us a good introduction to the area, but now we love it.'

'We have all sorts of plans for walks and beach trips,' Mrs Abernethy said, warming now. 'Four weeks here is going to seem all too short.'

They made polite farewells and continued the last few yards to the summit and the metal box where the visitors' book was housed, while Thea and Joe agreed with a few words that it was time to be heading back. Down on the flatter section of track once more, Thea wanted to refer to their meeting with the Abernethys, but Joe didn't say anything about it and she realised, not for the first time, I get much more wound up about all this than he does. I should take my cue from him . . .relax. . .but a lifetime of Pamela Carmichael's fussiness about secrecy had had its effects. There's a big part of me that's expecting this hike of ours to be all over town by tomorrow afternoon! she thought.

\* \* \*

Joe Stockwell threw down his paint-scraper in disgust and went to his chest of drawers to change out of stained jeans and an even filthier T-shirt into clean khaki shorts and a fresh white sports shirt. Stopping on his way through the chaotic sitting-room, he grabbed an olive-green sweatshirt and an electronic pager — the first in case it was cold on the beach, the second because he was on call. Climbing into his silver-grey Mazda, he barely bothered to warm the engine before gunning the car backwards down the drive and up along Whaler Street.

Life felt rotten today, he decided, and renovating quaint old cottages was for the birds. Last week, he had loved the place. The smaller of the two bedrooms was finished now, its floor sanded down and made a glowing golden-brown with several layers of sturdy polyurethane, and its walls painted cream and rimmed with decorative borders in blue tones that matched the gloss-painted wooden window-frames. A blue and cream Persian rug softened the floor, and eventually the still rather bare room would be filled with furniture gleaned from antique fairs or bric-a-brac sales and carefully restored. With cream curtains and some pastel-toned prints on the walls, it would be a rather pretty, feminine room. . .

But to what purpose? he asked himself today. It was four weeks since that hike up Pigeonhouse Mountain when he had almost found the words to ask Thea to marry him. Since then, no propitious moment had presented itself, and he was beginning to wonder now whether one ever would. Perhaps, after all, it was still too soon, or even altogether wrong. . .

He reached Wintooma Beach and flung himself across the sandhill, following the restless, rhythmic call of the surf. The wind whipped his hair across his eyes and the salt water breaking across his tanned bare feet as he walked was cold. Bringing that sweatshirt had been wise. He found the bracing air invigorating, though, as it buffeted his skin and filled his lungs.

How naïve he had been seven weeks ago to think that keeping his relationship with Thea a secret would be fun! He had realised pretty quickly that fun wouldn't enter into it, but he hadn't thought that the clandestine nature of their meetings would be quite so destructive. They didn't dare go to restaurants, or drive anywhere together in the same car. They couldn't shop together, go to Tooma's one cinema, or sit on his newly purchased outdoor chairs in the back garden.

He had never liked phone calls; he only used them to make brief, practical arrangements, and couldn't understand how some people loved to chat for hours with that hard circle of plastic pressed against their ear. If he liked talking to someone he wanted to *see* them as well, and, if it was Thea, *touch* her. Now that the Abernethys had left and Thea had moved into her grandparents' house, she wouldn't even let him visit in case a nosy neighbour saw them together.

Sometimes her caution angered him and it was all he could do to stop himself from saying petulant words that he didn't mean at all, Well, if that's the way you feel, why are we bothering to see each other in the first place? But he managed to bite these words back, and at other times he fully shared Thea's concern. Poor Peter Welland still hadn't got over that episode with Sister Jenny Thirkell, Thea's predecessor, and the whole town knew about it, or thought they did. The business had come close to ruining Peter's marriage, and was still having an effect on his career.

And while things between himself and Thea bore no resemblance to what had happened between Dr Welland and Sister Thirkell, it was an unpleasant reminder that this *was* a small community, things *did* get known and talked about, and consequences could spiral out of anyone's control.

I *must* keep on seeing Thea and I *won't* rush into asking her for a commitment out of frustration! he thought for the hundredth time. There has to be some way to throw in a red herring so that no one would dream of Thea and me having a connection. Should I invent a fiancée in Sydney? No, people would expect to meet her. A broken heart that hasn't healed? Not my style.

And then he thought of the answer. Not the perfect answer, not something he would particularly enjoy, but an answer all the same. . .just as the pager clipped to his shorts began to give off its insistent piping sound.

'So, is the doctor on his way in?' Glenda Watterson demanded as soon as Thea returned from making the call. It was just after lunch on a Saturday, a rather blustery April day that foretold very clearly the autumn storms to come. This time the pregnant woman had come in alone, getting a lift with a neighbour and leaving her husband with the older children.

'Yes, he should only be about ten minutes. . .but we know what he's going to say, so. . .'

'I know, lie on my left side with my feet slightly raised. If I've been told once, I've been told a dozen times.'

Glenda Watterson had reluctantly paid a visit to the obstetrician in Wannego, Dr Hill, and an ultrasound scan had confirmed Joe's suspicions. She was carrying not twins but triplets, and it was pretty clear that she had not yet fully come to terms with the fact. Joe had ordered her to rest, had begged her to stay under Dr Hill's care, and had suggested the possibility of spending the second half of her pregnancy in Sydney, but the tired mother of two had clamped her jaws grimly and

said that it was impossible. She had to stay here to look
after the two older children, and with the financial
constraints that triplets would bring she had to continue
with her part-time job as well.

Now she had come in with another episode of pre-
term labour, brought on by nothing more serious than
carting the family washing out to the clothes-line, it
seemed. Thea went to meet Joe as he came down the
corridor. She knew the sound of his car by this time
and had heard it pull into a parking space out the front.

He was very casually dressed, a look that suited his
rugged, outdoorsy frame, and his hair looked wind-
swept as if he had been on the beach.

'I think we have to make it clear to her that she
could lose all three of these babies if she doesn't take
this pre-term labour seriously,' Thea said to him,
without wasting words in greeting. She wanted to make
her point before they arrived in the room where Mrs
Watterson had been placed.

'You think she's not taking it seriously? Still?' Joe
returned, stopping Thea with fingers held lightly on her
forearm. As usual, she was intensely aware of his touch.

'Not the right kind of serious,' Thea said. 'She's
angry today. Really angry, as if it's our fault that this is
happening, and as if we should see that we're asking
her to do the impossible.'

It wasn't an unusual reaction in a patient. Hard to
deal with, though. Thea could see Joe considering his
approach as they covered the remaining distance to
Mrs Watterson's room. Thea had already prepared a
syringe and a dose of ritodrine, anticipating Joe's call
for the beta-mimetic drug, so he was able to inject it
straight away, ordering a repetition of the programme
of care and medication that had successfully stopped

the unwanted contractions several weeks ago. As anticipated, Mrs Watterson was to stay in overnight.

'But what are we going to do about you for the next five months, Mrs Watterson?' Joe asked her.

'I haven't got the time or the energy to think that far ahead, Doctor!' She glared at him, as if he should personally wave a wand and give her one baby instead of three.

'Well, in that case, let's think *one* month ahead. You'd probably be just about getting back on your feet by then, and back to normal.'

'What do you mean, back to normal? I thought you said——'

'Another episode of labour two weeks from now, say, and very possibly this time we wouldn't be able to stop it. Three babies born before they've got the slightest chance of survival. You'd need some time to recuperate after a major miscarriage like that, so——'

'You mean, I really could lose them? All three?'

'Yes,' he said briefly and bluntly. 'Not could. Will. In fact, you're lucky you haven't lost them already. . . Unless that's what you want. If so, you can easily make it happen. Just go on as you have been doing!'

Thea repressed a shocked gasp, even though she knew that Joe was being intentionally callous in tone and words. Mrs Watterson's rather coarsely moulded face had turned pale. She whispered, 'Of course I don't want to lose them!'

Joe's manner softened as he leaned closer, forcing the patient to meet his steady gaze. 'Then you *must* give up work, you *must* get help with the children and the heavy housework, and you *must* start planning for the strong probability that you'll spend the last few months of your pregnancy in Sydney, in hospital, on full bed-rest.'

'What about seeing Dr Hill? Do I have to do that?'

She looked up at Joe, who had stepped back now that his threatening performance was over. 'That drive up and down for office visits wouldn't be good for me, would it?' Glenda pointed out hopefully.

'No, true,' Joe sighed. 'No, you can continue as my patient. And when you go to Sydney —— '

'You said "if", didn't you?'

'I said there's a strong probability. So strong that we might as well treat it as a definite. You'll find that the specialist I refer you to there is a wonderful doctor and a very nice man. . . Or, if you prefer, I could refer you to a woman.'

'A woman?' Glenda Watterson looked rather sceptical about this revolutionary idea.

'Think about it,' Joe suggested.

Thea had found some magazines for Mrs Watterson to read, and after answering one or two more questions from her the doctor and nurse were able to leave. The corridor was quiet at the moment. Sister Drummond was on duty today, but she was assisting Dr Lister with a caesarean delivery in the small operating theatre. Sister Clinton had been called in for this as well, along with Dr Anderson as anaesthetist. There were two elderly men in residence at the far end of the corridor, too, each convalescent but needing several more days of hospital care and observation after returning from hospitals in Sydney, following major surgery.

Thea and Joe walked towards the hospital entrance together, enjoying the rare chance to be themselves. 'Was I too harsh with her?' Joe said, referring to his blunt words to Mrs Watterson.

'No, I don't think you were,' Thea answered him.

'I hated doing it.'

'I know, but she was in that stubborn state where she just wasn't going to hear the truth unless it was painted in the most terrible colours.'

'That's what I thought. Wanted to hear it from your perspective, though.' He touched her arm briefly.

They were approaching the entrance foyer now, where a receptionist was on duty. Thea said quickly and nervously, 'My mother and brother are coming down on Thursday to stay over the Easter break. Would you like to meet them?'

'Very much.' Brief words, spoken in his low, sincere tone. Thea felt very happy suddenly, and wished she could go and dance crazily on the beach. Joe smiled down at her, and their glances linked and held in a way that had her heart fluttering like a butterfly.

'I thought we could go out to dinner,' she said to him after a moment.

'Out?'

'Yes. I thought I'd take them down to Greerson's Bay for the day. There's a seafood restaurant in the town itself, overlooking the bay. . .'

'But that's sixty kilometres!'

'Saturday. Are you on call?'

'No, but——'

'You could meet us there, say you'd been into the shopping centre for hardware supplies. . .'

She trailed off, and then saw him nodding. 'Makes sense, I guess. Ridiculous. But it makes sense. And how am I to be introduced to your family? As a doctor from Tooma who's quite a nice chap?'

'Yes,' she answered him shortly, suddenly annoyed at the slightly mocking note that had come into his voice. Her happiness of a moment ago had gone. How else could she present him to her mother? Not as her boyfriend, when Mrs Carmichael would be sending a postcard from Tooma to Gran and Grandpa in Europe telling them all about the visit to their place. She went on crisply, 'Or do you want to have this come into the open, with all the consequences, such as my losing my job?'

'Of course I don't.'

'Then please don't act as if these awful games we have to play are just *my* idea!'

He opened his mouth with heated words clearly hovering behind his lips, then shook his head and clamped his teeth over the hot outburst. 'Sorry.' The word was ground out harshly, and his face was carved into a rugged frowning shape.

'I know it's awful ——' she began placatingly, but he cut her off.

'Yes, unbelievably so.' Then he turned to leave and she just heard his muttered words, 'I don't know how much longer I can stand it!'

He didn't say goodbye, and when Thea tried to she found that she couldn't. The words got stuck behind the lump in her throat.

'Well, it's a pleasant little town,' Pamela Carmichael said to Thea and David at seven on Saturday evening as the three of them sat down at their restaurant table. 'I've been through it before, of course,' she went on speaking in her usual rapid, nervous way.

She had lost a little weight, Thea decided, not pleased at the fact. Mrs Carmichael was really too thin already. 'When your father and I used to bring you children down here for holidays years ago. You probably don't even remember. We've got the fresh oysters to eat tomorrow, and renting the boat to explore the estuary was a good idea. That antique shop was fascinating and the white Victorian bedspread that you saw there was beautiful, but I'm not sure, Thea, why you were so keen on driving all that extra way when David and I had the long drive from Sydney only the day before yesterday.'

'Oh, this restaurant is really special, I've heard,' Thea said, off the top of her head.

It did look nice. They had a table overlooking the water and the long bridge that crossed the estuary of the Shale river. The blackboard specials looked mouth-watering, too, but there were restaurants as nice as this in Tooma. In short, Mrs Carmichael was right. There had been no very good reason to spend forty-five minutes driving on the winding highway down to Greerson's Bay, except that Thea wanted to be safely out of the Tooma area when she presented Joe at dinnertime. He should be here at any minute.

'This doctor,' her mother said, as if reading Thea's mind. 'Is he a special friend, or —— ?'

'No, no. He just mentioned that he had to come to Greerson's Bay today, so I invited him along. He's new in Tooma too, so I thought. . .' She trailed off once again. It sounded lame. I'm a rotten liar, she realised inwardly. I *hate* lying!

She wanted to be able to say, I met him in New Zealand and we fell in love and now we're both here, and it's so important that you all get along well, but *please* don't tell Grandpa! And that last phrase was the thing she couldn't say. After a lifetime of rebelling against such words, she didn't want to use them now, and she didn't dare to tell her mother that she was in love with Joe. Not yet. Not when she still had no idea where it was going.

She saw him at that moment, threading his way across the room to their table. From where she sat, he looked even taller than usual, dressed in pale grey trousers and a subtly patterned matching shirt and darker tie. He carried a dark sports jacket as well. Those slightly too long locks of his that so often fell on to his forehead were combed tidily today, and when he sat down Thea caught the faint masculine scent of a

musky aftershave. She realised in a bewildered way
that it was the first time she had ever seen him dressed
up for an evening out. Casual clothes suited him. . .
but these clothes suited him even better.

'Hi,' he said to Thea, giving an absent, enigmatic
frown, then he leaned across and shook hands with
both David and Mrs Carmichael, giving an open grin
and saying he was pleased to meet them.

Thea couldn't help wondering if it were really true.
Meeting someone's family was usually a big step in a
relationship. Had she pushed Joe into it? He had left
her in turmoil the other day with those ominous
muttered words about not being able to stand it. The
words had haunted her since, though she had said
nothing about them and neither had he.

On the surface, things had not been bad between
them. She had spent an evening at his place cooking
spaghetti, listening to music and, despite his protests,
helping him to strip the terrible old wallpaper from the
main bedroom. He had moved into the second bedroom now, which was utterly lovely after all his hard
work.

'You don't need to do this dirty stuff,' he had scolded
her, but she had told him truthfully that she liked it,
and it had been fun—the compact disc player in the
background, a break for some light beer, lots of very
silly conversation, and the sight, after two hours' work,
of the whole room stripped down to its marbled layers
of past paintwork.

'And that's another solid block of work—sanding
back the paint, before I can paint it freshly,' Joe had
sighed. 'Not to mention the tradesmen coming in to
put in the bigger window and the French doors.'

Two days later, he had phoned her at home for a
talk as well. That was unusual for him—Thea had
realised by now that he didn't like the phone—so she

hadn't chattered on, just talked briefly about her day and asked about his. So it hadn't been a terrible week by any means, on the surface, at least. Underneath, she was less sure. There were things they weren't saying to each other.

'You haven't been at Tooma very long, either, Thea tells me,' Pamela Carmichael was saying brightly now.

'No. Started the same day as Thea, as a matter of fact. Quite a coincidence,' He smiled across at her but his gaze didn't linger. Well, she wouldn't expect it to. After all, David and her mother weren't supposed to guess anything was going on.

Her mother. . . Mrs Carmichael seemed particularly twitchy tonight. Have I just forgotten how jumpy she can be, or is she getting worse? Thea wondered.

Mrs Carmichael asked anxiously about the menus and studied hers minutely, twitching the large folded sheet of paper in her hands and seeming very nervous about choosing the right thing. 'Do you think I'd like the king prawns?' she demanded of Thea, her eyes wide, as if it were a question of utmost importance.

'I'm sure you would,' Thea said in the soothing tone she had had to use habitually with her mother over the years. 'Have whatever you feel like. I've told you, it's my treat.'

'Your treat? Yes, that's right. But I didn't realise you were bringing us somewhere so expensive. Perhaps I should just have the onion soup and the salad.'

'Please, Mother. I didn't mean to make you think about the cost. . .'

Joe watched the exchange, which went on for quite some time before Mrs Carmichael could be persuaded to decide what she really wanted and order it without guilt or fuss. Thea was intensely aware of his scrutiny and, because she was nervous about the evening, it made her angry.

Why doesn't he talk to David, at least? she wondered impatiently. He's usually got more tact than this. Just *watching* us! And Mother is being so maddeningly fussy tonight. Worse than usual.

The atmosphere of the meal did not improve. Joe *did* talk to David, once their food had arrived, and the two of them seemed to get on well, but Mrs Carmichael continued to be anxious and twitchy, and Joe continued to study her exchanges with Thea closely so that the latter felt she was being judged.

'I'm expecting a baby within the next few days,' he said after finishing dessert and coffee. 'So I'd better get back.'

'A baby? Then you're married?' Pamela Carmichael put in, taken aback.

'Sorry. . . A patient's baby, Mrs Carmichael,' he laughed, but Thea was embarrassed.

Why did Mother have to get flustered and anxious about every tiny thing? And was Joe just using Carol Skinner's impending baby as an excuse to get away early? Mrs Skinner's due date *was* yesterday, but Dr Fane had been seeing her for most of her pregnancy, and he was on call. He could easily deliver the baby if it decided to come tonight.

Hiding her doubts, she said a friendly but very casual goodnight to Joe and watched him leave the restaurant with his usual capable strides. Mrs Carmichael suggested that they leave as well.

'I hate driving so late at night. It's too dangerous!' was her reasoning, so Thea hurried through the berry soufflé she had not yet finished and David downed — with difficulty — the strong and sticky mint liqueur that he had ordered. At eighteen, the sophistication of a liqueur was still a novelty.

Mother used not to be so nervous about driving at night, did she? Thea wondered on the way home.

In the passenger seat beside her, Pamela Carmichael twitched constantly, pressing her right foot into an imaginary brake pedal on the floor and gasping a number of times as they rounded sharp bends in the road, although they were travelling at a speed that was perfectly safe.

What an exhausting day! Thea decided as she fell into bed an hour later. I wish I hadn't gone to all that trouble to have Mother and David meet Joe! It was a pointless disaster. . .

But the next afternoon, though, Joe had told her something that made her feel very differently about the evening, and very thankful that it had taken place.

# CHAPTER SEVEN

'COULD you come round this morning?' Joe said over the phone.

'Well. . .my mother and David are still here,' Thea answered uncertainly. She had been surprised to hear Joe's voice and was even more surprised at this invitation. He knew her family wasn't leaving until Monday afternoon.

'Yes, I know that,' he was saying. 'But it's important. I need to talk.'

'All right. I can be there in fifteen minutes, if ——'

'Yes, do,' was all he said before hanging up the phone.

She made an excuse to her mother and David — something about seeing if the newsagency was open, to get the Sunday papers — then hurried out of the house, unable to squash fears of an unpleasant scene to come. He couldn't choose a morning like this to tell her that he didn't want to see her any more, could he?

Arriving at his cottage, she was nervous and it showed. He drew her in and took her to the enclosed veranda, pouring her coffee at once and saying nothing to reassure her. His face was very serious — that medical manner which suited him so well but was scarcely designed to make her feel good. He hadn't kissed her this morning either.

'Thea, has your mother lost some weight since you last saw her?'

It was the last thing she expected to hear. 'Yes. . .a little. She's never been overweight, though,' she answered haltingly.

'No, and you've also told me that she's always been the nervous, fussy type.'

'Yes.'

'Again, though, is it getting worse?'

'I'm certainly noticing it more. Are you suggesting a difficult menopause? Hormone replacement therapy?'

But he ignored her questions. 'She was very twitchy last night, too. Couldn't leave the salt and pepper shakers alone. . . Look, I think she should see a doctor?'

'You?' Thea was still bemused and uneasy.

'No, not me. Here.' He pulled a pad of paper towards him, and Thea saw that the pages had the letterhead of his medical practice at the top. 'This will serve as a referral, if she likes, or she can go to her own general practitioner who may recommend someone different.' He scribbled a note and a name, then looked up again. 'Dr Alan Freeman. He's an excellent endocrinologist, and if I'm right your mother is going to need one. I think she has Graves's Disease.'

Thea rose numbly, knocked over her coffee and didn't even notice. His words had shocked her so much that she couldn't even speak at first. When Joe reached quickly for a cloth and a sponge to mop up the brown puddle of coffee that was spreading on the tablecloth, Thea paced the length of the enclosed veranda, then, finding words at last, she said, 'I. . .I have to get some air. I have to think.'

Without even considering the fact that her visits to Joe's were supposed to be discreet, she opened the door that led from this room out into the back garden and fled down the short flight of steps, pacing the mown square of lawn. She didn't see Joe's neighbour Eileen McCredie out in her own backyard, running a hose over her rows of vegetables. She didn't see two pretty wooden tubs of rust-red chrysanthemums that

Joe had recently put in to flank a wrought-iron garden seat either.

Mother has an over-active thyroid gland, she was thinking. Can it be true? How can Joe know from. . .? But he's right, the symptoms are there. Why didn't I see it before? Because she's always been like that. But no, he's right, she *has* been getting worse over the last couple of years and I noticed myself that she had lost weight. Her eyes, too. . .

Thea remembered how they often seemed to stare, with a startled slightly bulging quality. But lots of people have prominent eyes and a nervous manner. He can't be right! I would have seen it myself months ago, wouldn't I? I'm a nurse! Mother, too, she would have suspected.

The thoughts churned round and round, till finally she calmed down enough to take stock in a rational way. Joe might be wrong, but he probably wasn't. Those closest to a person with hyperthyroidism, or Graves's Disease, as it was also called, often did miss the tell-tale signs long after they were quite evident to a disinterested professional. The changes happened gradually, and, if someone had always been of a thin, nervous disposition, family members often said, as Thea had said to herself, Mother's getting worse.

Thea would have to persuade Pamela Carmichael to see a doctor—a task which might well take some coaxing and bullying. Then, if Joe's suspicions were confirmed by tests which these days were relatively straightforward, there were three potential forms of treatment. Anti-thyroid drugs, a subtotal thyroidectomy—the removal under surgery of most of the gland itself—or radio-iodine treatment. A doctor considered several factors before deciding which of these treatments was best for a particular patient. Once the treatment was carried out, Mrs Carmichael's outlook, like that of almost all people with thyroid problems now, was very good. Still.

'It has been a shock, hasn't it?' said Joe gently, coming out to her and leading her quietly back into the house, with a wave and a smile over his shoulder to Mrs McCredie that Thea did not see.

'Yes. I still don't want to believe that you're right.'

'I may not be.'

'But she must see a doctor.'

'Yes. Then a simple laboratory test ought to tell you for sure. The serum thyroxine level will be raised and you'll have an unequivocal diagnosis.'

'She doesn't like doctors much.'

'She married one, didn't she?'

'I think that's part of the problem!'

They laughed, and Thea was able to relax a little. 'Last night,' she said, 'I thought you were rude, the way you kept studying her, staring at her. . .'

'I *was* rude. I knew it. It was terrible not to be able to drive home with you and explain then and there. But I couldn't spring something like this on you without being as sure as possible that I wasn't misreading the signs.'

'I should have seen them myself. After I came back from New Zealand, or. . .'

'We're unfair to the people we love. Alzheimer's Disease, lupus, thyroid problems. People often just dismiss it as, "Dad gets more difficult every week", without seeing that there's more to it.'

'I must go home straight away and talk to her about it!'

But he put a restraining hand on her arm and chafed the lightly tanned skin gently. 'Not yet. Drink your coffee. You're still a bit shaky.'

'I should have seen that it wasn't just her usual fussiness.'

Joe sat quietly opposite Thea and let her talk it out, touching her hands now and then, reminding her to drink the coffee that replaced the one she had spilt. He wondered if she even realised that it was a different mug! He wanted to keep her here with him all day, just have a silly, friendly sort of time, but he knew it wasn't possible, and after twenty minutes he judged her able to drive with enough of her mind on the road.

At the door, she returned his kiss absently and he held himself back although he wanted to pull her close and tight and almost crush her in his arms. She seemed so vulnerable this morning, with her fine hair and slim build, dressed in grey-green trousers and a top in broad stripes of white and the same grey-green. He loved it that after all her concern over the secrecy of their romance she could forget about it totally in a situation like this when her mother's health was what filled her mind.

He had planned to do the usual prudent thing, which was to say goodbye at the door and remain in the house as she hurried quickly down the street to her car, parked in some distant anonymous location, but today he saw that the pink Citroën was pulled up brazenly in front of the house for all to see. She had been worried, then, just from his manner over the phone. Also, when he tried to release her to shut the cottage door between them, she clung to him and he quickly surrendered, walking with her down the front path to the waiting car, and letting her cling to him as she clearly needed to do.

'Hope you have a good talk with her,' he said softly, and she nodded, then impulsively he kissed the serious, sensitive mouth one last time. He watched her as she drove away. . .then turned to see Eileen McCredie coming around the side of her house, still with hose in hand.

'Hello,' she called out to him, with a friendly wave. Grey hair floated around her forehead in the light breeze.

'Hi,' he returned. She was a friendly old soul, a widow, with not quite enough to do all day long, not malicious in intention by any means, but. . . He hadn't told Thea quite how close an eye Mrs McCredie kept on her neighbour's business.

'Was that the old doctor's granddaughter I saw just driving away?'

'Yes,' Joe nodded. And did you see me kiss her as well? he wanted to ask, but didn't.

'She's a nurse up at the hospital, isn't she, taking over Rosemary Sinclair's job for the rest of her maternity leave?'

'Yes, that's right.'

'She looks like a lovely girl.'

'She is.'

'I see her when I go up there for Senior Citizens.'

'Right. . .' He knew it was best not to say too much. Making an excuse about a phone call to make, he went into the house.

Actually, he *did* have a phone call to make. That red herring he had thought of some days ago — it was beginning to seem rather necessary. Looking up a number quickly in the local telephone directory, he dialled, waited for a moment, then said, 'Hello, Jessica?'

Ten minutes later, he had arranged to take part in the alternative healing workshop, that the health-food-shop owner had been touting for some time now. It took place in a couple of weeks. And he had also arranged for Jessica Lewis to come over for lunch, which he would make sure took place in the back garden under the shade of that old apple tree, complete with beer, laughter and even an arm or two draped casually around Jessica's well-rounded shoulders. He suspected that Eileen McCredie would be sitting out on her back porch for most of the afternoon. . .

'Have you made a doctor's appointment yet, Mother?' Thea asked into the phone as she stood in Tooma Community Hospital's front office.

It was Tuesday afternoon at four o'clock and the senior citizens' activity club that met in the hospital's recreation-room every week was just ending. It was always a noisy time, and if Thea had remembered about it she would have delayed making this call for ten minutes. The group enjoyed itself thoroughly, but several of its members were a little hard of hearing so the pitch of conversation tended to be rather loud.

Thea, after giving her mother a morning's grace, and then unable to reach Mrs Carmichael at home at lunchtime, was snatching the chance to try again now, while things on the ward were fairly quiet.

'Not yet, dear. I lost the. . .' Mrs Carmichael's words were drowned by a new surge of noise as several more people came out of the recreation-room and began making their way down the corridor and through the foyer to go home.

'You what? Sorry?' Thea raised her voice.

'I lost that referral thing you gave me.'

'Well, go to your own doctor. That might make you feel more comfortable about it. You like him, don't you?'

'Yes, but I heard that. . .' Again her words were drowned but Thea could tell from the tone that it was some thin excuse.

'Mother,' she said fiercely. 'You *must* go as soon as possible. I'll ring again tomorrow afternoon. If you call for an appointment now, you'll get to see Dr Chalmers tomorrow morning, and I want to hear a full report on what he has to say. Or if you find the referral, try the specialist directly.'

Mrs Carmichael began talking again and this time Thea frankly didn't listen. In fact, she *couldn't* listen. Just outside the office door stood Eileen McCredie who, at seventy, was a good ten or fifteen years younger than the senior citizens who came to the activity club. She did duty as a volunteer helper each week and was well liked by even the oldest of the patients, a rather crotchety woman who had already seen the end of her ninety-first year.

These two were talking together now, and since old Miss Netherglade was extremely deaf Mrs McCredie was almost shouting. 'I *said* she had lunch at his place on Sunday.'

'Oh, yes?'

'Out in the garden. He barbecued.'

'They argued?'

'*Barbecued*. No, they didn't *argue*. They were getting on very *well*. She'd be a good *catch* for a country *doctor*. She's making a lot of *money* with that *health-food shop* of hers, and running these *workshops*.'

'Workshops? With tools?'

'No, no. You know, it's that new sort of thing. They call it a workshop these days. We'd just have called it a course of study in our day.'

'In *my* day, she wouldn't have. . .' Miss Netherglade began in her quavering yet spicy voice, but at that point they moved out of the foyer and into the April wind and could not any longer be heard. Most of the other elderly people had left now too.'

'So you see how difficult it is.' Mrs Carmichael was audible once more.

Thea said through clenched teeth, 'Just make the appointment, Mother!' and slammed down the phone, then felt bad and almost redialled her mother's number to apologise for speaking that way.

She didn't do this, though. She had already been away from the ward for long enough, and in any case she didn't trust her voice at the moment. Eileen McCredie was Joe's next-door neighbour, she knew, and the elderly woman had been speaking of Joe and Jessica Lewis — 'getting on very well' spoken with an arch intonation that hinted at more than friendship.

'How ridiculous! She must have got it wrong!' Thea snapped impatiently under her breath. 'Joe wouldn't. . . Jessica couldn't be. . .'

But a doubt remained and it didn't help two hours later when Dr Stockwell whisked in and out to see a patient so quickly and busily that he didn't even manage to say hello to Thea. Three months ago, she would have thought that Jessica Lewis's predatory tactics wouldn't have a chance at succeeding with any man, but Charmaine Tandy's aggressive attitude to her own affair had shown Thea that the ruthless approach could work. Not in this case, though, surely!

She got home at ten-fifteen that night, still fighting against doubt and distrust. Dialling his number and finding that her hand was damp against the hard plastic receiver, she almost put the phone down again. What am I going to say? she wondered. She hung on, though, listening to the insistent ringing until realisation finally dawned that he wasn't at home.

Dropping the receiver back in its cradle, she was just about to go and make a cup of hot chocolate. The night was chilly. . . It would calm her down. . . There was no reason to feel miserable. . . Then suddenly, just as her hand came away from the instrument, it rang, startling her, and she snatched it up and put it to her ear, sure that it was Joe.

So sure, in fact, that her 'Hi!' was breathless, tender, caressing and vulnerable.

'God, who are *you* expecting?' came a strident yet lazy feminine voice.

It took Thea several seconds to recognise the caller. Finally, 'Hello, Charmaine. This is a surprise.'

'That's obvious. You sounded as if you'd been waiting by the phone all evening for him to call.'

'For who to call?'

'Whatever male charmer you were obviously expecting *me* to be. Sorry to disappoint!'

'I'm not disappointed, Charmaine. I wasn't expecting anyone. I'd just put down the phone from ringing my mother,' Thea lied, hating it.

'Of course,' Charmaine agreed silkily. 'Anyway, I didn't ring just to gossip. I've got some news.'

Now Thea could hear a controlled excitement and eagerness in the other nurse's tone. 'Good news, obviously,' she said, trying to make her voice sound warm. It was hard to do, since she had good reason to dislike Charmaine Tandy quite a bit. She hated clouding her life with open hostility, though, so she made as much effort as she could.

'Well, *I* think it's good news,' Charmaine said. 'And so does Ewan. We're engaged!'

'Congratulations to both of you, then.' It wasn't what she needed to hear tonight.'

'Thanks.' Charmaine accepted these congratulations as her due. 'Obviously we can't set a date for the wedding until we know when his divorce is coming through. . .'

'I wouldn't have thought so, no.'

'But as soon as we do you'll be one of the first to hear about it, and to get an invitation.' Thea tried to say that she would look forward to this, but failed and instead said nothing. Charmaine went on hastily and a little nervously, 'Listen, I know what happened two months ago was pretty ghastly for you. I'm sorry about that. I'll make it up to you, I promise. Once we're married I can ask Ewan to ——'

'It's all right, Charmaine. I'd rather you didn't, thanks.'

'No? All right, then, that's great. I'm glad you understand. I was just crazy back then, crazy to get Ewan away from that woman. I would have done *anything*.' She said this with a note of pride, as if it testified to the strength of her love. 'But now it's all worked out for the best and everyone's happy. I'm over the moon! Ewan is incredible!'

She gushed on for several more minutes, not noticing—or perhaps just not caring—that Thea's replies were minimal. Everyone's happy, the younger nurse was thinking. Does that include Trish Baxter, I wonder? Finally the conversation came to an end, with more promises of an invitation to the wedding—which was going to be an elaborate one—and help from Ewan about anything at all if Thea ever needed it.

She felt drained when she had put down the phone, and went to the kitchen now positively craving the hot chocolate she had been planning when Charmaine telephoned. She had just set the milk in its saucepan on the stove when a knock sounded at the door, and this time it *was* Joe. She pulled him into the house then he fell into her arms with a groan of need and she saw that he was exhausted.

'That's right,' she remembered. 'You were up half the night with Mrs Souter's delivery, weren't you?'

'Since three,' he nodded. 'And I haven't stopped since.' It was now well after ten. 'We're swamped in this practice. Greg needs to take on another partner.'

'But he's only recently taken on you.'

'I know. The problem is, poor Peter Welland has

been losing patients because of the wretched business with your predecessor. From what I can gather it was scarcely his fault, but blame attaches itself all the same. People say there's no smoke without fire, and it rocks his own confidence as well. He says he should have seen that she wasn't behaving normally and needed help.'

'Joe,' Thea came in desperately, 'this may sound ridiculous, but. . . I don't *know* what this scandal was between Dr Welland and Sister Thirkell, and I think perhaps it's about time I did.'

'You don't *know*?'

'I didn't want to, at first.' She told him how she had felt two and a half months ago after the whole business with Charmaine and Ewan and Trish Baxter. 'I was like someone who's just eaten three wedges of Black Forest torte. I didn't even want to *hear* the word chocolate. That's not a very good comparison, but you know what I mean.'

'I think you should hear it now,' Joe said.

'I know I should. But can you kiss me first?' she asked weakly. She always felt so good in his arms.

He laughed. . .and the milk boiled over on the stove. Switching off the hotplate and leaving the mess to do what it liked, Thea told Joe, 'I don't feel like hot chocolate any more, anyway.'

'Still feel like a kiss. . .?' His tone was caressing and hopeful.

'Strictly a therapeutic one, Doctor.'

'Been a long day?'

She thought of Charmaine's announcement over the phone, of her mother's reluctance to face the probability of her illness, and of Eileen McCredie's overheard words about Jessica Lewis. 'Just kiss me, Joe!'

He did, and in his arms she wondered at first why she had ever doubted things between them. He had pulled her on to a roomy floral couch so that they were entwined together and she was aware of the heat in him and of every firm, supporting muscle. She splayed hungry fingers out to run them through his thick, glossy hair then arched her back a little so that she could feel his whole length pressed against her.

The touch and taste of his lips was familiar to her now, but that only made his kiss stir her more deeply. Tonight, as his lips made a trail of fire down her throat to nuzzle at the open neck of the casual dress she had slipped into when she got home, she knew that she was very close to going much further than this with him.

They had never spoken of her inexperience, but she knew that Joe had guessed by this time that he was the first man in her life. His kisses were always passionate but never forceful or demanding. Soon, though, the time would be right for them to discover the full depth of their connection to one another and she found that she was nervous about it, unsure of how it would happen and how she would feel about it when she still didn't have any spoken seal of commitment from him.

This nervousness must have communicated itself to him tonight. He pulled away from her far sooner than he would have done several weeks ago. In fact, Thea suddenly realised, he had been doing this quite a bit of late — turning his body away quite abruptly just as she was beginning to forget herself utterly in his arms. Now he sat for several long seconds in silence with closed eyes while she watched him, frowning and unsure, when only a few minutes ago all her doubts had seemed foolish.

Opening his eyes finally, he caught her wide-eyed gaze, pressed his palms to his face briefly, then said gruffly, 'Sorry,' without quite making it clear to her what he was apologising for. He went on, 'I was going to tell you about the business with Dr Welland, wasn't

I?' He seized on the subject as if it was a welcome distraction and Thea tried to do the same, although she gladly would have postponed any talking that wasn't about their two selves.

'I think you should,' she managed to say, 'since it seems to be affecting our lives.'

'Not a long story. I'm not going to make it a long story, anyway. The nurse whose position you took over——'

'Jenny Thirkell.'

'Yes. She developed a crush on him.'

'Plenty of nurses do that.'

'This time it got out of control. She became obsessed with him, came to believe that he was in love with her although he was married and had never shown her anything more than ordinary friendliness. She started reading secret messages into any instructions he gave her, or any conversation they had at all. She began ringing him or his wife at home at all hours of the day and night, pleading and occasionally abusive. He told her time and time again that he had no feelings for her, tried to get her to behave more reasonably and more discreetly.'

'What an awful situation!'

'Then he did a foolish thing. He agreed to go to her house for dinner, planning to tell her once and for all that it was all in her mind and she should get professional help, but of course she only interpreted it as a sign that he *was* interested. While at her place he was called to the hospital, but she didn't believe the call was genuine, thought he was abandoning her. She followed him to the hospital and pulled out a gun, started threatening him, Sister Drummond, a patient. . . Finally Peter talked her into handing over the gun. Turned out it wasn't even loaded. She was sedated overnight and her parents came the next day

to take her back to Sydney with them. Apparently the
same sort of thing had happened twice before, only
less intensely.'

'That's awful. . .and very sad,' Thea whispered.

'The good news is that she's under treatment now
and is apparently doing very well. . . But yes, it is sad,
and many people believe that Peter must have encour-
aged her. There are all sorts of versions of the story
going round that are much wilder than the truth, but
Peter told me all this himself, and he has been deeply
shaken by it. I believe he was as helpless in the situation
as he says. His only fault was, as he says, in not seeing
sooner that she was developing real psychiatric
problems.'

'And of course some people see a story like that as a
piece of juicy gossip. . .'

'And are waiting for more scandal to mushroom out
of the Tooma community hospital,' he nodded. 'That's
what your grandfather and the rest of the hospital
board are afraid of, I suppose.'

'The thing is certainly widely known,' Thea said.
'Jessica Lewis mentioned it to me the time she came in
with those cut feet.'

'Hmm, Jessica,' he said absently, narrowing his eyes
in sudden thought.

Thea waited for him to say more about the attractive
blonde, but he didn't. It seemed to take him a while to
rouse himself from the train of thought that had
gripped him and she couldn't help wondering if it was
Jessica he was thinking of.

She wondered if she should offer him something to
drink. It was getting late. How long did he want to
stay? All night. . .'Is your car parked outside?' she
asked, speaking the thought as it occurred to her.

'Yes. It shouldn't be, should it? Sorry, I wasn't
thinking about the wretched neighbours and what tales

might go round.' He got abruptly to his feet and paced the room impatiently. 'Thea, I loathe this! I find myself hating Peter Welland sometimes because if he hadn't been so damned *pleasant* maybe Jenny Thirkell would have found some other outlet for her feelings and we'd have been able to let this thing between us grow in the right way. As it is. . .'

'I know. I'm sorry I asked about the car,' Thea said, too quickly. 'I wanted to ask you too. . . Today I overheard Eileen McCredie——'

But he wasn't listening. 'Look!' he said, wheeling round to face her. 'Maybe you should leave Tooma, go back to Sydney.'

'Sydney? But that's——'

'It's four hours away. I know. We'd see each other less, but at least we could be open about it when we did. . . No! Forget it! It was a crazy idea!'

He lunged across the room, making her gasp with surprise, and took her in his arms, burying his face hungrily in her hair and her neck. His touch melted her at once and she wanted to cry with relief. The idea of leaving, sprung on her like that, had appalled her.

'I love it here, Joe,' she whispered to him. 'The small hospital, where I get to see everyone from tiny babies and their mothers to fascinating old people. And I love the beaches and headlands and the mountains up to the west. I'd be so happy if it weren't for——' She broke off, then continued rapidly, feeling the words only as she spoke them. 'In some ways it's not even the secrecy. I wouldn't mind other people not knowing, if *I* knew, but I feel we're not going anywhere with this. We haven't got a shared understanding about what's happening. I overheard something today. It upset me.'

'What, Thea?'

'Eileen McCredie said that Jessica Lewis had lunch at your place on Sunday.'

She couldn't help making the words sound like an accusation and he reacted, pulling away and staring down at her, his face twisted into an unreadable expression. 'I was going to tell you about that. . .' he said slowly.

'Were you?' It came out through tight lips. 'I mean, I'm sure there's nothing to tell. It's not that I think. . .'

'Don't you? Good! I'm glad.' He was angry now. She could tell by the way he held his shoulders, rigid and wary.

Plunging on, she knew even as she spoke that she was only making things worse. 'Joe, you can't blame me for being suspicious. It's obvious that she's more than interested in you and that she's the kind of woman who'll go after what she wants if she thinks she's got the sightest chance of getting it. If you had her to lunch she must have seen that as encouragement.'

'What are you suggesting?' he growled ominously, in a tone she had never heard him use before. 'That you don't trust me?'

'Of course I trust you,' she said shrilly, feeling quite out of her depth. 'It's other people I don't trust. It's this whole situation. If. . .if we could decide to get engaged, so that I could——'

'Decide to get engaged?'

'Yes. Is that such a terrible idea? It seems to me as if it would be quite useful.'

'Useful?'

'Yes! Stop repeating everything I say with that questioning expression as if——'

'Thea, I'm not agreeing on an engagement because it would be "useful". I'm sorry. I don't think we should talk any more tonight. Thea, love, I'm *tired*!'

He spread his hands helplessly and couldn't say anything more. Watching her standing there, her small elfin face crumpled and uncertain, he hated the whole situation. He shouldn't have come round here tonight, not when he was so tired. And when he realised that *she* was tired too. . .and he should have guessed that she *would* be tired since he knew she was concerned about her mother and no doubt sleeping badly as a result. . . He should have suggested they put on some music, have a hot drink and not talk about anything much at all.

Instead, they had got mired down in a whole lot of stupid stuff about Jessica Lewis, Peter Welland. . .and now she wanted a useful, sensible decision to get engaged. He should be in seventh heaven that she was thinking about that sort of commitment but he wasn't, couldn't be, not when it had been spoken of in anger and confusion, and not when he had had such different ideas about how it should come about.

He looked around at the tidy, open-plan living area of this spacious house. James and Hester Carmichael's was a very pleasant place, although furnished a little fussily for his taste, but it wasn't the setting he had imagined for the sealing of his commitment to Thea. At the end of a long meal in Shellhaven's finest restaurant, in the middle of a romantic walk along the beach, at his cottage in the soon-to-be-completed main bedroom after they had made tender and passionate love. . .these were the pictures that filled Joe's mind when he thought of Thea and what he wanted to say to her about their future.

Now, for the moment, all those pictures were spoiled and he was angry—with her, a little, but mostly with himself. It had been stupid to think that giving the town some gossip about himself and Jessica could help where it really counted. . .with Thea. He had planned to tell Thea about it too, of course, but Eileen McCredie, typically, had got in first, and he *did* feel angry with Thea for not trusting him enough to know that there had to be an explanation.

Rousing himself from the regretful churning of his thoughts, he stepped towards her, intending to kiss her once before saying goodnight. It would be best for both of them just to sleep off this unfortunate night and start again in the morning. He was about to touch her lips when she spoke, her mouth small and her eyes, such beautiful grey-green jewels, very wide and round. 'Would it help if. . .? Would you like to. . .to stay the night?'

Knowing that she was inexperienced and that she was nervous about it, and knowing from his own past relationships—just two of them, as he wasn't a promiscuous man by any means—that tonight would be the worst possible night for what she was suggesting, he said very gently with his arms around her, 'No, Thea. I think it's best for tonight if I just go home.'

# CHAPTER EIGHT

'I SAW the specialist yesterday,' Pamela Carmichael reported to Thea two days later, over the phone.

'Good!' Her tone contained a wealth of emotion.

'He's almost certain that Dr Stockwell is right.'

'The thyrotoxine test has to go to the pathology lab, I suppose?'

'Yes. He expects the result later today, and I'm to come in and see him again straight away.'

'And then?' Thea prompted, sensing that there was more to come.

'He wants me to have surgery.'

'Which you will, of course.'

'I'm very nervous about it,' Pamela Carmichael gabbled suddenly, in a flurry of the anxiety that was characteristic of hyperthyroidism. 'A subtotal thyroidectomy. What if they take out too little?'

'That's *very* unlikely, Mother,' Thea scolded.

'It's scheduled already. For next week. He wanted it done as soon as possible. In the meantime, if the test does come back with the result he expects, he's going to put me on Lugol's iodine. . .is that what it's called?'

'Yes, that's right.'

'To start bringing my thyroid function back to a normal level.'

'Don't worry about the surgery. If anything, the surgeon will take out too much of the gland, because that's safer than too little.'

'Too much? That doesn't sound——'

'In which case the worse that can happen is that you'd have to take a *small* amount of medication to replace the lost thyroid function. Now please tell me the exact date so I can arrange to come up.'

'Should you? Take time off work? What would your grandfather —— ?'

'I'm coming up. Don't even *suggest* that I'd do anything else!'

'Of course I'd love it if you came. I've never liked hospitals, or understood them. . .'

They went on talking for some time, and Thea's mother gave her details of when she'd be in hospital. It was Thursday afternoon, and Thea had had a morning shift today. She sat curled up on the couch, dangling the phone cord lazily in her hand and watching heavy rain falling outside. It dripped from the trees and gurgled in gutters, and created a cosy sort of feeling indoors. . .or it would have done if Thea had been feeling happy enough to be cosy.

'Please thank Dr Stockwell for me, won't you, Thea?' Mrs Carmichael said as their conversation drew to a close. 'This Dr Freeman seems very good, and he says I'll feel like a whole new person after the surgery. I realised I have been feeling so very anxious and upset at everything lately. My heart seems to race and I can't sit still. I'm tired all the time, and I always have the feeling that so much needs to be done and I'll never get through it. He says that almost all of that should lessen dramatically after the operation and I'll feel a whole new sense of calm.'

'He's right,' Thea answered. 'I *will* thank Dr Stockwell for you and. . . I love you, Mum,' she finished as she felt a sudden surging wave of love for this often difficult parent.

'Do you, dear? Thank you. Oh, goodness! What is the cat doing? I must go!'

'I'll ring again as soon as I can to tell you my arrangements for coming up.'

'All right. Goodbye.'

After putting down the phone, Thea went over to the windows and watched the rain unseeingly for several minutes. Her mother had asked her to pass on thanks to Joe. Did this mean she should try to get hold of him on the phone? Or wait till they saw each other? He would be swamped at work this weekend, she knew. Dr Fane was off to a conference and Joe was taking his on-call time, as well as extra office hours, which would still be going on at this moment.

'I'm not agreeing on an engagement. . . I'm sorry,' he had said two days ago, in a voice heavy with frustration and weariness.

'It's my own fault,' Thea murmured aloud to the raindrops. 'Why did I say it? Why did I ask him about Jessica? I'm so stupid and tactless! If only I'd had more experience in these things.'

Experience. Sexual experience. Was that what it came down to? Joe hadn't wanted to stay the night on Tuesday, and if she was honest with herself about it she knew she was glad. It would have been a terrible time for such a thing, when they were both tired and when the evening had been so fraught with misunderstanding. Was it a short-lived hiatus in the unfolding of their relationship. . .or the shape of things to come?

She had seen Joe twice yesterday at the hospital and once today, but each time another nurse or a patient had been present and it hadn't been possible even for a special glance to pass between them. As a doctor should be, Joe was concerned about his patients.

Mrs Watterson was still not resting enough, apparently, a terminal cancer patient being treated at home needed more and more pain medication, Mr King was back with them after a month of therapy in Wollongong and he was so anxious to be home again that he was trying too hard with his programme of exercise and occupational therapy. . .

I won't ring him this evening, Thea decided. He doesn't like talking on the phone. When he's got time, if he wants to see me, or to talk, he'll ring.

He did, twice, briefly, over the weekend, saying so little that she still had no idea about how he was feeling inside. It was obvious that he didn't have time to see her. He had been up most of the night on Friday and Saturday, and his voice was husky with weariness.

Then on Tuesday afternoon Thea found herself in the pink Citroën on her way up to Sydney, as Mrs Carmichael's surgery had been scheduled for tomorrow morning and she was to be admitted tonight. Rosemary Sinclair, the nurse who was to return from maternity leave in a month's time — and Thea had no idea, at this stage, what her own plans were after that — had agreed to take two of Thea's shifts and the rest would be covered by Judy Clinton and Barbara Dawes, another member of the hospital's nursing staff.

On Monday night she had tried to phone Joe to tell him that she had successfully arranged her schedule to go to Sydney, but he hadn't been home, and on Tuesday morning she hadn't wanted to try his office, so on her way through Tooma to the highway she had left a note in his letter-box, leaning out of the car window to deposit it and hoping that Eileen McCredie was occupied with something other than her neighbour's business today.

Outlining the timetable for her mother's surgery and thanking Joe again for his perception about her condition, Thea had finished, 'I'll be back on Sunday in time for my afternoon shift, then I have days off from Wednesday till Friday.'

That last sentence only hinted at what she wanted to say far more directly: Please can we get together, do something fun and relaxing and romantic? Please tell me that it's still all right between us!'

The five days in Sydney were long ones. Typically Pamela Carmichael's thyroid condition made her extremely nervous and anxious about the surgery. Fortunately, Thea was able to stay with her for several hours after she had been admitted. On Wednesday, after the surgery, Mrs Carmichael was very groggy and unresponsive, but Thea managed to meet with the endocrine specialist, Alan Freeman, and. hear her mother's story from a professional angle.

'I decided on surgery for two reasons,' he said. 'Firstly, your mother seems to feel very uncomfortable about hospitals and medical treatment in general.'

'Yes, she's always been that way,' Thea nodded, glancing at the sleeping form, still attached to several tubes and with a neat dressing around her neck like a pearl choker. 'I think the fact that my father was a doctor only made it worse. She feels intimidated and out of her depth.'

'Yes, I wondered how much of that was the illness.'

'No, it's part of her personality,' Thea said.

'Which is why it took a stranger to recognise the picture,' Dr Freeman came in. 'Although Dr Stockwell is an excellent diagnostician in any circumstances.'

'Yes. . .'

'Which is why he'll make a superb general practitioner, and at the same time be utterly wasted in such a role.'

'Wasted? He loves it!' Thea couldn't help putting in firmly and indignantly.

The specialist, a neat, pale man in his late forties, smiled cynically. 'I know he does. The man doesn't have a particle of ambition. I urged him to try my own field, but——'

'He *is* ambitious,' Thea insisted. 'His ambitions are

different, that's all.' She thought about these ambitions briefly, relishing them because they matched her own: to be as good as he could in his field, to have a well-rounded life that left room for leisure and replenishment, to have time to care about other people. Then, because it was too dangerous to keep talking and thinking about Joe, and because her mother was the most important person in her thoughts just at this moment, she went on quickly, 'But you said there were two reasons you'd decided on surgery.'

'Yes. The gland had become somewhat enlarged. Not enough to present as an obvious goitre — that might have alerted you or your mother to the presence of the disease earlier — but enough to give her some discomfort in swallowing. Apparently she put this down to being the sort of lump in the throat that one gets when one is nervous — and of course she felt nervous constantly. Mr Tottenhouse performed the surgery. He was extremely pleased with how it went. He's very experienced with this particular operation and I think it very unlikely that there will be any complications. I'm speaking of bruised nerves in the vocal cords, or bruised or excised parathyroid glands.'

'You didn't tell Mother too much about complications and so on. . .'

'No, she said she would prefer not to know those details. I discussed the three treatment options with her. . .' Thea knew that this meant surgery, radio-iodine treatment and anti-thyroid drugs '. . .And surgery was the one she felt most comfortable with, because of getting it over with quickly.'

'When will she be discharged?'

'Barring anything unforeseen, in about six or seven days.'

'Will she be able to travel a few days after that? I'd

like to have her down with me to convalesce for a week.'

'Take the journey carefully. Have her see Dr Stockwell at least once, and have her see *me* as soon as she gets back.'

Dr Freeman had to leave at this pooint, but Thea was satisfied with what she heard. She stayed at her mother's bedside for another hour, studying the face that she had so rarely seen in this relaxed state lately. Towards the end of the hour, Mrs Carmichael stirred and opened her faded blue eyes, smiling faintly as she registered the presence of her daughter.

'Don't try to talk,' Thea said quickly, squeezing the thin hand whose fingers were spread lightly on the stiff white hospital sheet. 'The operation is all over now and everything went fine. I've talked to Dr Freeman and he's very pleased, and so is Mr Tottenhouse.' She spoke softly and soothingly, and saw Mrs Carmichael's faint nod. 'Just rest, and I'll be in to see you again as soon as I can tomorrow. David is coming for visiting hour tonight.'

She left the hospital after this. It wasn't her own Mount Royal, but South Sydney General, where Joe had spent several years. It had lovely old grounds and an air of importance with its large ambulance bays and frequent signs showing the way to its many departments. Very different from the small community hospital in Tooma, where there was such a small handful of staff and where most of the patients had familiar faces.

Do I want to come back to a hospital like this — perhaps *this* hospital — when I've finished in Tooma? Thea asked herself as she walked to her grandmother's distinctive pink car.

The answer, soon found, was, No! She loved the small-town atmosphere of the South Coast, with the extra bustle and life that tourism brought to the region in the summer months. She loved the beaches and the mountains to the west. She loved having the chance to follow a patient's progress closely from admission to discharge and to run into that same patient at the post office a few weeks later and see that they were doing well.

And Dr Freeman is wrong about Joe! Wanting to be a good GP and a fulfilled person *is* ambitious! she told herself.

She and Joe as yet had made no plans. Her nervous attempt the other day to talk about the future and an engagement had been rebuffed, and yet he hadn't said that he wanted to stop seeing her. When her temporary position at Tooma ended in five weeks' time, he would stay on. . .but what did he want *her* to do?

The question had to drop to the back of her mind for the rest of the week. A get-well card from Joe arrived at the hospital for her mother, and a postcard, saying little but ending with, 'All my love', came for herself. It was nice that he had taken the trouble to write, thoughtful of him, and tender, but it didn't really tell her a lot about how he was feeling.

She spent every visiting hour with her mother, and the time in between was taken up in looking after Mrs Carmichael's house. The latter's illness had made her tired, and when Thea looked closely at the tranquil three-bedroom brick bungalow with its surrounding garden she found that neglect stared her in the face.

Ivy was running wild, roses had died for lack of water, a vegetable patch was completely overgrown but when weeded it yielded several kilograms of squash and tomatoes. Dust had felted into thick carpets beneath beds and on top of curtain pelmets, and kitchen cupboards needed a complete inventory and overhaul.

David, being a teenager and a male one at that, had been somewhat oblivious to all this, but he promised very earnestly to do more around the house till their mother was on her feet again.

'Just till then?' Thea queried in her bossiest older sister voice.

'No,' he growled, a little ashamed, and annoyed at Thea at the same time. 'I suppose I should tackle the garden from now on.'

'Just the heavy part. Mowing the lawns, and that sort of thing. She'll enjoy some pruning and planting.'

'I don't mind doing it, OK? I just never think of it.'

Thea rapped her knuckles gently on his head as if to suggest that it was made of wood, and they were friends again. He would be Mrs Carmichael's nurse for the first few days after she came out of hospital and before Thea drove to Sydney again to bring her down to Conway Bay, but in this area she knew that he would do a good job and that no lectures were necessary.

Thea was tired by the end of the week, though, after all her work, and more tired once she got home to her grandparents' house in Conway Bay. Getting up early to do some last-minute chores around her mother's house, wangling permission to pay Pamela Carmichael a last visit out of regular visiting hours before driving south, and then the four-hour drive itself. . . There was just time to freshen up, grab a bite to eat, change into her blue striped uniform and head back to Tooma for her afternoon shift at the hospital.

Dr Stockwell wasn't on call tonight, she found when she looked at the roster by the phone in the nurses' station. The list read Dr Fane for tonight and tomorrow, and Dr Welland for Tuesday. Evidently the former was back from his medical conference and was making up the time, and it was he who came in that evening to check on Glenda Watterson's condition.

'Yes, I'm here again.' The pregnant woman had nodded ruefully to Thea, seeing the nurse's expression. 'I'm going to Sydney by ambulance as soon as they think it's safe for me to be moved. I've been so stupid about this!' She gave a brief sniffle and her eyes brimmed. 'When Dr Stockwell came round about a week and a half ago and saw me on my feet at the ironing board doing all Chris's shirts and trousers he said I'd be back here within a week and he was right.'

A week and a half ago, Thea thought after she had left Mrs Watterson. Was that the night Joe had come to her place at the end of the evening? No wonder he'd been tired and dispirited, then! It didn't do any good to realise this now, of course. . .

Dr Fane came in several times the next day as well, once to check on patients, once to treat a case of food allergy, and twice for other minor emergencies. On Tuesday, it was Dr Welland's turn and, now that she knew the story of him and Sister Thirkell, Thea could see the strain and premature ageing in his face. He delivered a baby that night, and though all went well Thea saw him hesitate twice — over the question of an episiotomy, and over the significance of the baby's slightly below normal Apgar score — when a doctor of his experience would normally have had no doubts. She had heard a rumour that he was thinking of leaving general practice and moving away from the area to go into medical administration. It was probably a wise idea.

Confidence was a funny thing, she mused on the way home, a little tired, at ten that night. She had thought, after their time in New Zealand, that being near Joe and seeing him often would confirm what they each felt about the other and would lead to an understanding about the future, but after two months her doubts were greater than ever.

That Tuesday night at last, though, just after she got home, he telephoned. 'Thea?'

'Hi!' Her voice trembled a little, betraying her weak relief at hearing his voice.

'Is it all right that I haven't called?' he asked at once, his voice low.

'No, it *isn't* really,' she told him, feeling this quite strongly all of a sudden, in spite of the cards he had sent.

'I know,' he acknowledged. 'Well, I'm calling now. I wanted to — to ask about your mother, and just to hear your voice.'

'It's been over a week, Joe.'

'I needed a break. A chance to think. I thought you did too, perhaps.'

She made a non-committal sound, unable to speak suddenly.

'How is your mother?' he was saying now.

'Doing well.' This was a safer topic. 'She should be going home tomorrow. She has no phone in her room but I've rung David each day since I've been back and he gives a good report. She's coming down here on Friday. I'll be driving up to collect her.'

'Sounds good. I'm glad she had Tottenhouse for the surgery. He's just about the best, and Dr Freeman is razor-sharp.'

'He thinks *you* are! He told me he wanted you to specialise in his field.'

'Specialise?' Joe dismissed the idea. 'Deal with one gland or one organ? I like the whole human organism, as well as its habitat, thanks, and its parents and its kids and its cousins. . . But listen.' His voice dropped to its most earnest pitch. 'I hate listening to you down a wire. I. . . I want to see you quite badly. I would have rung on Sunday, but I knew you'd be dog-tired. I hate just ringing when I *can't* see you. Are you tired now?'

'I was, but ——'

'Forget it, then.'

' — talking to you, I've revived.'

'You have? Can I come and get you, then? We'll go for a drive. Look at the moon over Conway Point. Come back to my place for some supper. I bet you haven't been eating properly.'

'No, I haven't, I suppose, but ——'

'Then it's settled,' he interrupted, as if her nutritional requirements were the only important thing.

She laughed, felt better than she had all day, and agreed. The fact that they might be seen together in his car didn't even occur to her.

He was on her doorstep so quickly that she suspected he had broken the speed limit and *knew* he hadn't stopped properly at the stop-signs as he crossed the highway. He took her in his arms at once, right there on the front terrace, and the taste and texture of his lips against hers was so delightful that she never wanted his kiss to stop. It had to, of course, and soon he was helping her into a dark rust-coloured jacket and running down the steps ahead of her to start the car while she locked the house.

As they drove, she was intensely aware of him and when he reached across and pulled her closer so that she could nestle against the warm bulk of his shoulder she felt a deep happiness bubbling in her like some rich chocolate syrup.

He stopped the car at the gravelled parking area on top of Conway Point and they got out and walked to the edge of the headland, from which they could see the swell of the waves rippling into Conway Bay like long, well-toned muscles. It was a chilly night and the stars in an incredibly clear sky twinkled with a cold, glittering light. Even the almost full moon looked cold, and Thea wondered if up towards the Budawang Ranges there could even be an early frost. She didn't feel cold, though. How could she, with Joe's arms never letting go of her for a second and her own holding him just as tightly?

'I missed you terribly while you were away in Sydney,' he told her, his voice throaty with emotion. 'We had that bad night before you left. . . That's really why I didn't ring over the past couple of days. I wanted to wait until the bitter taste of it faded, and until we could see each other. Can this be a fresh start?'

'We don't have to agree on that, do we?' she whispered to him. 'It just *is*, isn't it?'

'Yes. . .' He kissed her, his fingers trailing around her neck and through her hair then falling to her hips to hold her against him while he nuzzled her throat with his firm, hot lips.

Thea felt a mounting need and desire, not only physically — although that was intensely strong and urgent — but emotionally as well. She wanted to know that she belonged to this man as completely as a woman could. . .to know that her skin belonged to him because every inch of it had known his touch, that her breathing belonged to him because he had called forth a complete, panting response from deep within her diaphragm, that her heart belonged to him because she had given it freely as a part of the gift of her body.

She wanted to say all this to him but could not find the words even in her mind, let alone frame them with her lips to speak aloud. Instead, she sighed and melted against him, moulding herself to his longer, more muscular form more closely than she had ever dared to do before. He groaned and tore himself away, leaving an icy trail suddenly where a moment ago his lips had been so warm. It was the wind, she realised, evaporating the damp mist of sweat that their heat together had generated.

'Let's go home,' he rasped heavily.

'Home?'

'Not to your grandparents', to my place. I've got something I want to show you.'

'To show me? Oh. . .all right, yes, that'd be good.' With an effort, she sounded enthusiastic, but his sudden twisting out of her arms and this murmured suggestion of something to show her. . .it wasn't what she had been hoping for.

But perhaps this was her own problem, she decided as they drove — in silence — away from Conway Point. Her hazy dreams of lovemaking had always been seamless, and she had trusted that when the moment came it would be right, but perhaps that sort of thing only happened in films. . .or in fantasies. Perhaps the reality was always more pedestrian, a disappointment. . .

By the time she reached his cottage, she was feeling much better. He had begun to tell her an amusing story about the tradesmen who had been working on the cottage recently, and this reminded her that her physical attraction to Joe, powerful though it was, was far from being the only thing of importance in their relationship. He had relaxed now, too, and when he led the way into the kitchen, past his tightly closed bedroom door, suggesting Irish coffee and chocolate cake, she happily agreed.

'Choose some music while I get it made,' Joe suggested, and Thea spent a contented five minutes looking through his compact disc collection, which contained everything from opera to heavy rock, before settling on the mellow tones of a female jazz singer.

'Now look at this trick,' Joe said, coming in and

laying a tray of cake and mugs on the battered old coffee-table. He went to a wall switch, turned a new knob there and dimmed the lights, also new ones, recessed into the ceiling above the fireplace. 'Isn't that neat?'

'It's wonderful,' Thea teased. 'I can barely see the stains in the carpet and the tears in the wallpaper now.'

'Meaning I've got my priorities wrong?' He glared, pretending to high indignation.

'Well. . .'

'The electrician was in last week doing some work in the bedroom, so I had him do the lights in here while he was at it. . . But come and look.' He pulled her by the hand across the central corridor, threw open the door of the bedroom and switched on the lights. 'You see, I happen to think that bedrooms are the most important, that's all,' he whispered, holding her close.

Thea gasped. 'It's finished!'

'I've been working on it like crazy since Greg came back from the conference and I got some days off. Do you like it?' The question caught in his throat a little, as if the answer was very important to him.

'Like it? It's a miracle!'

She had seen the other bedroom, of course, and had loved that as well, but this was even better. A double set of colonial-style French doors, made of wood and tooled glass, opened on to the veranda to the east and the enlarged southern window was perfectly proportioned for the room. The floor was sanded and refinished and on the third wall stood a matching antique wardrobe and high dressing-table, while against the fourth wall was a large double bed, its wrought-iron bedstead painted a glossy black.

But it wasn't so much these features that Thea noticed. It was the details: the old washstand, expertly re-stained, with a big china jug and bowl, the painting on the wall above the bed that captured the beauty of the Budawang Ranges as only a skilled local artist, with a love of the area in his bones, could have done, and the antique cotton bedspread with its intricate white-on-white design.

She recognised it as the one she had seen and loved that day at Greerson's Bay with her mother and David. She had told Joe about it afterwards and realised that he must have made a special trip down to Greerson's Bay to find it and buy it.

'Oh, Joe!' she breathed, her throat tight.

If Joe had had any doubts about her reaction to the room, the emotion in her voice as she said his name would have set them at rest. She loved it! Thank goodness! He had made a mental note of everything she had said lately that gave clues as to her taste, asking casually about the name of that antique shop in Greerson's Bay, making sure he committed it to memory and going down there at the first opportunity.

She hadn't suspected, he knew, chatting away — that night when she helped to strip wallpaper — about the tranquillity of Victorian-style bedrooms and how white in a room helped to make it feel so pleasantly light and airy. It was fortunate, he thought, that she hadn't expressed a preference for red flock wallpaper with pink lace curtains and a green floral nylon bedspread . . .but he would have got them for her if she had.

Now there was something very important that he wanted to say to her and he thought he had set the scene right, timed the moment, made her feel warm and at ease. Not a proposal of marriage. That idea was best left alone for a while, he had decided during that painful yet important breathing space over the past two weeks when they had barely seen each other.

No, this was something different, equally important, very right. . .

'Is it the sort of place,' he said huskily as he led her gently out of the room, leaving the light on this time, and the door open, 'where you'd like to spend the night?'

Thea turned to him, unable to speak. She buried her face in his shoulder and felt his mounting heat as they sank down to the couch together, their limbs tangled. Now she felt no uncertainty and only the smallest thread of nervousness, which he soon cut with his assured yet incredibly gentle and sensitive touch.

For half an hour they stayed on the couch, drinking the heady cream-topped coffee and eating the rich cake, while the music Thea had chosen played out its slow, seductive rhythms in the background. They laughed a little, talked a little, kissed a lot, and then, at just the right moment, he led her back to the bedroom where he peeled her clothes away from her body by the light of a low lamp.

Lying in the now rumpled bed, she watched him undress, the muscles in his shoulders and back rippling as he pulled off his shirt, and his thighs incredibly long now that they were no longer clad in jeans. Then he came to her, switching the lamp even lower so that only a soft golden glow lit the shining glaze of the jug and bowl on the washstand, and at last she felt his skin against hers and knew the full range of its textures — deliciously roughened by hair on his hard chest and as tender as soft kid at his untanned hips.

Their lovemaking took a long time and Thea blessed his sensitivity and patience until she lost all power to think about anything but the moment and the frenzied detail of his hands and lips exploring every contour of her body in the semi-darkness. Then came the final surging of his passion as they clung together, their breathing coming in a matched undulation of gasps and cries.

Afterwards, as they lay still, there was no sense of the experience being over, finished with. They lay together, murmuring a few words then slipping into a warm doze in which each other's touch lulled them deeper and deeper.

Later. . .much later—or only a little? She didn't know—he slipped out of the bed and turned off the lamp then came back to hold her again in a velvety darkness that made their closeness seem even more complete. They slept again, until Thea was awakened very gradually by his hands sliding around her and finding her tender breasts, cupping them and caressing them until their budded tips ached and burned with need.

She turned to him, knowing that her quickened breathing echoed his, and ready to feel and respond to his passion all over again. This time, exhausted and replete, they slept deeply and she didn't awaken until morning light was strong in the room. . .along with the smell of something burning.

She opened her eyes to find Joe sitting on the bed beside her, watching her face, and said to him dreamily, 'What's that I can smell? Coffee, but something else as——'

'Damn!' He jumped to his feet. 'The toast.'

She wakened more fully and found the navy silk dressing-gown he had laid on the bed for her, slipping her bare limbs into it, wrapping it across her body and fastening the tie at the waist before going out to the kitchen. There, she had to laugh at the sight of him wildly opening doors and slatted windows to dispel the blue undulations of smoke that filled the room.

'Your fault!' he said, turning to her with a teasing grin.

'Really? How long were you watching me?' she returned with mock-indignation.

'I couldn't bear to wake you.'

Thea saw that he was dressed and fresh from the shower, with tendrils of hair on his neck still dark and wet the way they had been the very first time she had seen him that afternoon beside the hotel pool in Christchurch.

'It's nearly eight-fifteen and I have to leave,' he said. 'I need to drop in at the hospital then get to our office and be ready to see a patient at nine.'

'And I don't have my car,' she realised.

'Exactly. Otherwise I wouldn't have woken you at all. I made coffee in case you wanted to stay and eat breakfast then let yourself out later when it's quiet. It's about three miles to your place, but. . .'

'Yes, I could walk it,' she agreed. 'It's a lovely day.'

'The toast I was planning to eat on the run. I'd invite you to share some, but. . .'

Neither of them mentioned in direct words the fact that, however she left his house it must be done discreetly. In the end she decided to skip the coffee, dress quickly and accompany him.

'How about going out the new French doors?' he suggested quietly, and she did so, knowing why he had suggested this.

The doors opened on to the opposite side of the veranda from Eileen McCredie's house and she could probably sneak around the front and get discreetly into his car. This was accomplished successfully, and they drove up the street. A hundred yards from the hospital he stopped again and said with a helpless expression, 'If you get out and start walking, I'll pick you up on Conway Bay Road after I'm finished, then I can drop you off at your grandparents' place on my way to the office.'

She nodded and said lightly, 'Sounds good.'

This time, it didn't work out so well, though. Turning

as she heard a car slowing behind her on the road fifteen minutes later, Thea found Jessica Lewis leaning cheerfully out of the window. 'Need a ride?'

'No, thanks. I'm enjoying the walk.' An innocent enough lie until Joe's car appeared over a rise, slowed briefly. . .and sped up again to pass her with a cheery wave from the driver. He couldn't stop and pick her up when, as he must have guessed, she had just refused Jessica's offer.

'OK, then,' Jessica was saying. 'Oh, was that Dr Stockwell? He's signed up for the workshop this weekend. I must ring him to see if. . .' She didn't bother to finish. 'Well, it's a lovely day. Enjoy your walk.'

'I will.'

And Thea did, for the most part, although a small voice inside her said that her sense of completeness after last night was very dangerous. Re-living those heady hours in his arms, asleep and awake, felt wonderful. . .but Joe hadn't spoken of a commitment between them and he had never once, Thea realised now, said that he loved her.

# CHAPTER NINE

'DID your mother have a comfortable journey down from Sydney?' Joe asked Thea on Saturday morning.

They were snatching a moment for some private conversation at the nurses' station while Barbara Dawes, the other nurse on duty, was answering a patient's bell. Thea answered, 'Yes, it went well. She's taking things very quietly so far. Talking still irritates her neck and throat, but she already says she's feeling better than she had felt for a couple of years.'

'Yes, once those symptoms disappear there's usually a new lease of life. I was hoping I'd be able to come and see her. Would that be possible?'

'Of course, Joe.'

'I feel a professional interest, you see, since I was the one to ——'

'I understand,' she assured him. 'Why don't you come over tonight for dinner?'

'Dinner?' He made a face. 'I'd love to, but I've got this workshop of Jessica's from noon to eight. Odd tims, I thought, but apparently this *incredible* alternative healing guy from Sydney needs to sleep late.'

Thea laughed. His imitation of Jessica Lewis's manner and vocabulary was subtle but exact. They hadn't talked much about Jessica lately, apart from laughing about the other day and Thea's unplanned walk home. 'If it had been raining I would have stopped for you, Jessica, or no Jessica,' Joe had assured her.

'If it had been raining, I wouldn't have got out of the car in the first place, hospital or no hospital,' Thea had retorted.

He had phoned her on Wednesday night to ask her if she would spend the evening again on Thursday, which she did, bringing a seafood casserole she had made during her day off. A dreamy day, Thursday had been, with a long walk on the beach, shopping for the casserole ingredients and cooking as she listened to some of her grandparents' classical records. She couldn't wait to see Joe that night. . .

And it had been as wonderful as she could have wanted — a lazy dinner, a glass of wine, and bed, where already her nervousness of Tuesday night was quite gone and she was ready to explore and discover more and more about their passion together. On Friday morning she had left his cottage early as he had done himself, wanting to ensure that her grandparents' house was immaculate clean and well organised for her mother's stay, with fridge and pantry fully stocked and everything arranged for Pamela Carmichael's comfort.

Then in the afternoon and early evening she had made the tiring double journey between Conway Bay and Sydney and had had a very quiet hour in front of television with her mother once they had safely arrived back. Now it was early Saturday morning and she was at work again.

'After dinner, then,' she suggested to Joe. 'Will you be eating at this workshop?'

'I gather a nutritionally perfect meal will be served at some point.'

'Well, you'll have to leave room for nutritionally *imperfect* dessert with us,' she teased, and left it at that.

The morning was uneventful at the hospital until eleven, when a familiar face appeared: old Mr King, in the charge of his middle-aged daughter, who was clearly worried about him and made irritable because of this. Mr King had made an almost complete recovery from his stroke, the only handicap that remained being a slight slurring of his speech if he tried a particularly difficult sentence. Today, though, it wasn't stroke symptoms that had brought him in.

'His bronchitis is just *terrible*!' Joanne Aitkens, his daughter, reported, glancing at the old man. 'I arrived for a visit on Thursday and found him with it, and still intending to go out fishing. He just *wouldn't* come in to the doctor yesterday as I wanted him to, but then he had such a bad night last night. . .'

'We'll call a doctor in to have a look at him,' Thea promised.

She rang Dr Lister, who was on call today, then settled Mr King into a comfortable chair to wait. He did look and sound terrible, wheezing and coughing and fighting for breath. The strong cough syrup that his daughter had purchased for him seemed to be making him drowsy and when Thea asked about it she found it was one that had a rather high alcohol content.

Listening to Mr King's chest fifteen minutes later, Dr Lister recommended that he be admitted for a few days, given some oxygen and started on antibiotics to combat any further bacterial complications. Thea knew that pneumonia was a real danger and was frequently the cause of death among the very aged, if it was not caught by antibiotics in time.

'He's Dr Stockwell's patient, isn't he?' the grey-haired doctor asked Thea in a low voice as Mr King settled himself listlessly into his new bed.

'Yes,' Thea nodded.

'I'll phone him to tell him what's happened. He'll probably want to check on the old man himself some time today.'

'I should think so,' Thea agreed. She didn't tell Dr Lister that she knew Joe was at Jessica Lewis's workshop and would not be answering his phone at home today. He had a pager with him in case of dire emergency, but since he was not actually on call less urgent messages would simply be recorded on his telephone answering machine.

Talking to Joanne Aitkens in the corridor once Mr King was comfortably settled, Thea tried to sound optimistic, but there was something in Mr King's manner that made her apprehensive and she knew Dr Lister had detected it as well. He seemed to have lost heart. Remembering how keen the old man had been only a few weeks ago, to work hard on his physiotherapy, get home and become independent again, she asked Mrs Aitkens, 'Has anything happened in his life lately? Any changes in circumstances?'

Joanne Aitkens, who was clearly worried but did not seem overly perceptive, said vaguely, 'No, nothing that I know of. An old friend of his died a couple of weeks ago, his fishing partner Maurie Crabbe, but at Dad's age his friends are dying all the time, and he's lost two brothers and a sister over the past five years. Of course it saddens him, but. . . Trouble is, he won't accept the fact that he's old. Just will not give up fishing, for a start. I told him I was going to sell his rods. "What's it going to be, Dad?" I said. "Fishing or living?"'

'Perhaps one is what gives meaning to the other,' Thea murmured.

'Pardon? Oh, yes, he's always loved fishing. That's why he retired down here eighteen years ago. Hated giving up driving a few years back, but he still manages to get about. Old Maurie used to drive him to all sorts of out-of-the-way coves and beaches, take him out in the boat. Funny that Maurie should be the first to go. He was only seventy-two and Dad's eighty-four. But no, I don't know of anything that's happened to him lately. His dog is fine. We're all fine, my brothers and our families and me.'

Thea didn't say much after this. Joanne Aitkens couldn't see that something as simple as fishing with a friend could be important enough to make a difference in Mr King's life, but Thea suspected that it was the loss of this that the old man was mourning. Losing a friend and losing one's main interest all in one blow. . .

I'll tell Joe about it tonight, she decided. We may have a losing battle on our hands here. . .

That afternoon, after she finished work at two, partly to shake off the sadness she felt at Mr King's loss of heart, Thea took her mother on a drive to Granite Falls and Boyd Lookout, two scenic spots about half an hour's drive from Tooma and Conway Bay. She was a little worried that the trip would be too much, but Pamela Carmichael seemed keen on the idea and they had a lovely afternoon, taking pictures of each other atop the smooth, dramatic curve of the falls and sitting on the edge of the escarpment at Boyd Lookout while they ate cake and drank tea from a Thermos flask.

On the way back, with dusk already descending, they stopped at a Chinese take-away in Shellhaven and bought an appetising assortment of dishes which they ate at home with music in the background.

This has been the best time I've had with Mother in years, Thea decided as she stood at the kitchen sink to wash the small assortment of dishes afterwards.

Making coffee an hour later after watching the television news, she realised she had not yet told her mother that Joe was dropping in this evening, and suddenly she felt stupidly nervous about breaking the news. As it happened, though, she didn't have to. Just at that moment, and a good fifteen minutes before she was expecting it, Joe's knock came at the front door.

'Did the workshop finish early?' she asked him as she ushered him in.

'No.' He looked a little tense and tired. 'I got called in to the hospital.'

'Not Bert King?'

'Yes.' He let out a sigh. 'He's all right. Got very agitated and confused and they thought they'd better have me come in, since Dr Lister doesn't know him. They wondered if it had been another stroke, but I don't think it was. He seems to be failing rapidly in all sorts of respects. Those lungs aren't good.'

'I had a talk with his daughter.'

'Yes, not brilliantly sensitive, is she? Maurie Crabbe's death has really taken the wind out of him.'

'Oh, she told you about that?'

'*She* didn't. I read it in the death notices, and knew from what Mr King had said about Maurie that he was important.'

'Mrs Aitkens told me she had threatened to sell her father's fishing rods.'

'Great!' He was scathing. 'So that's what he meant this evening when he was talking about them. When she comes in for visiting hour tomorrow, can you ask her to make it clear to him that she *won't* sell those rods?'

'Of course. But now you must come in and see Mother.'

'Lead the way. . .'

'So you missed out on the end of the workshop,' she commiserated, not with entire sincerity, as they went into the sitting-room together.

'Don't worry, there's still tomorrow! What I *did* miss out on, though, was dinner.'

'What a good thing we had take-away Chinese, then. There's heaps of left-overs. Dr Stockwell has dropped by to see how you are,' she told her mother, before ducking into the kitchen to warm the Chinese and bring out the coffee and a light beer for Joe.

The two of them seemed to be getting along well
when she got back. They weren't talking about medicine or thyroid conditions at all, but about this afternoon's outing, and Thea was pleased to hear her
mother say, 'It was the nicest afternoon I've had in a
long time.'

'Yes, those falls are magnificent, aren't they?' Joe
agreed. 'Most waterfalls have a flat shelf at the top
where the water plunges off, but that huge polished
curve at Granite Falls is spectacular and unusual. It's
the granite. It doesn't weather into flat shelves, it
weathers into rounded forms.'

'It was frightening.' Mrs Carmichael shivered. 'Such
a gentle slope at first, then getting steeper and steeper.
I could see myself today stepping too far, slipping and
going all the way over.'

'So could I,' Thea came in. 'That's why we stood so
far back we barely saw the falls at all!'

Joe laughed, recognising the exaggeration. 'When I
was there, the friend I was with *did* lose her sunglasses
over that curve, so you were probably wise to play it
safe,' he said.

'Wise, but not very adventurous,' she agreed.
Inwardly, she was wondering when Joe had been to
Granite Falls, and who was 'the friend'. Jessica Lewis?
Why had he never mentioned the expedition? Was it a
recent one? She wanted to ask, but didn't. Joe received
his cold beer gratefully and ten minutes later the
Chinese food, which he tucked into hungrily. Again,
Thea wanted to ask him whether the workshop had
been worthwhile, but again she didn't. Later, perhaps,
if they got a chance to be alone.

Joe was asking Mrs Carmichael about her hospital
experience now, listening and nodding intently at her
answers. She had liked Dr Freeman, had had confidence in him, had had confidence in Mr Tottenhouse

but *hadn't* liked him much, had found the nursing staff helpful and approachable.

'I must thank you,' she told Joe now. 'For seeing what was happening to me. I suppose deep down I knew something was wrong but I managed to put it down to any number of other causes — menopause, general ageing, natural worries about my children growing up and what they would do with their lives. As Thea has probably told you, I've never been a very relaxed person anyway, never an easy person to live with.'

'Mother. . .'

'Dorothea! I'm not an easy person. I know that.'

'You'll be a lot better now,' Thea answered lamely, wondering with a little shame just how careless she had been over the years about letting her irritations show.

'This is good Chinese,' Joe came in cheerfully, to Thea's relief. Typical of him to sense tension and try to break it. 'Did you get it from the Golden Lotus?'

'No, the Fortune,' Thea said.

'The Fortune is better, then,' was Joe's conclusion. 'I'm afraid the Golden Lotus has lost my patronage.'

'You're a regular, are you?' Mrs Carmichael laughed through a still tender throat.

'I'm a busy bachelor. What can I say?' He spread his hands helplessly.

He did not stay long after this, turning down Thea's offer of coffee or a second beer. 'But would you mind walking me out to the car?' he asked her, then turned to Mrs Carmichael. 'A couple of questions I need to ask about one of our patients. I won't keep her long.'

'I'll turn on the television again,' Mrs Carmichael answered. 'There's something I want to watch at nine.'

Once outside, Thea and Joe stood by the car in a spot where they were partially screened from the road by the dense foliage of a tall shrub. 'She seems to be doing very well,' he said.

'Yes. She's like a new person. It's wonderful. . . Did you want to ask me something about Mr King?'

'No.' He smiled teasingly. 'Wanted to kiss you, actually. *Didn't* want to do it in front of your mother.'

'No. . .' She turned her face up to his and felt the delectable nuzzling of his lips which so quickly drew a tingling response from her.

'Can we see each other while she's here?' he asked, speaking seductively against her mouth.

'I. . . I don't think so.'

'No, I thought not.' His voice was terse with a disappointment that she felt just as much.

'She'd be so anxious if she knew I was doing something that would displease my grandfather. And I shouldn't stay out here too long either, Joe.'

'I realise that.'

'But tell me about the workshop.'

'Oh, it was good. . .interesting. . .fine.' He shrugged offhandedly. 'Rubbish in some parts, kernels of truth in others. Must we talk about it? When does your mother leave?'

'Friday. David is coming down to pick her up.'

'Can you come round on Friday night?'

'I have a morning shift, so yes.'

'One the next day too?'

'Yes, so I'll have to get up early.'

'In that case, we'll have to go to bed early. . .' He kissed her, until a car going past shone its headlights glaringly on them for a second as it rounded a bend. They froze.

'That wasn't Sister Drummond's car, was it?' Thea said nervously.

'Relax, Thea.' But he drew away from her all the

same and she knew it was out of respect for her nervousness about being seen.

Aware of her mother waiting inside and aware of the fact that she had just agreed to spend another night with Joe when he still hadn't told her in outright words that he loved her, Thea felt a familiar misery and doubt stealing over her, and couldn't help voicing her fears and feelings in the worst way. 'Was Jessica there today? At the workshop, I mean.'

'Of course. It was her show.'

'Did she continue her attempts at a romantic conquest of your person?' She tried to make it a flippant question, but of course it didn't work. He knew her too well now and could see that a part of her was seriously undermined by the idea of someone pursuing him with so much more assertive experience and confidence than she had herself.

'Hey!' he challenged her now. 'This isn't jealousy, is it?'

'Of course not, but I——'

'Look, this is going to make me angry, Thea!'

'You went to Granite Falls with her, didn't you, while I was in Sydney?' she rode over him.

'Yes, and if you want to know it was a horribly embarrassing afternoon.' He had narrowed his eyes and tensed his shoulders. 'She's not very subtle.'

'So why did you go? Why did you sign up for her wretched workshop?'

'To give the town something else to talk about, of course! Haven't you heard of the term "red herrings", Thea?'

'You could have told me.'

'I intended to, but then the business of your mother's illness came up. Eileen McCredie saw you at my place that Sunday morning so once you'd gone I quickly got on the phone and invited Jessica to lunch. You were

far too preoccupied at that stage to be interested in my
amateur attempts at creating a playboy image?'

'Amateur?'

'Yes!' he glared. 'I'm not very good at it, you know.
I hated the idea of Jessica Lewis slobbering all over me
and I didn't want to hurt her, either, if she decided she
could be serious about me. You've got no idea how
many fascinating insects I had to pretend to find that
afternoon at Granite Falls so I could peer down out-of-
the-way cracks in the rock in order to get away from
her arms. You would have laughed if you'd been there.
I wish you could laugh now, for heaven's sake!'

Reluctantly, she managed a smile. 'I suppose I
should have done the same. . .started going out with
Grandpa's garage mechanic, or something!'

'Might have helped,' he growled.

'Well, it's less than a month now till Rosemary
Sinclair comes back and then we'll be free of this,' she
answered him, trying to speak lightly. 'What's going to
happen after that, do you think?'

'I don't know, Thea,' he answered heavily. 'I really
don't know. You'd better go in, hadn't you?'

'Yes. Mother might be wondering what's happened
to me.'

'I'll see you on Friday, then.'

He bent and kissed her briefly, then turned and
climbed into his car. She watched until he drove away,
answering the last wave he gave before the car sped up
along the road.

Well, I've cleared up the question of Jessica, Thea
told herself as she walked up the step that led to the
terrace and the front door. She's a red herring. Nothing
to fear. And I've angered him by being jealous and
demanding. And he doesn't know what's going to
happen to us when I finish at the hospital. I don't
know, either. I want *him* to have the answer!

Inside, her mother turned from the television. 'He's a very thoughtful man.'

'Yes, he is.'

'You're not in love with him, though, are you, Thea, or anything silly like that?'

For the first time, Thea saw a return of her mother's old manner, not heightened by an over-active thyroid now, but Pamela Carmichael's normal rather nervous personality.

'No, I'm not in love with him,' Thea lied.

'I'm glad of that. Don't let yourself become so, dear, if there's any inkling of it. Doctors make terrible husbands. They're never concerned when the children are sick. They've seen everything before, rashes and fevers—they don't take your fears seriously. The hours they keep wouldn't be so bad except that they don't think they need to phone to let you know. They think you'll assume they're at work when often you find yourself thinking, He could be out there, lying in the road and I wouldn't know. I'd just think he was held back at the hospital. It was so ironic that your father should die of heart failure in his own bed after all those nights I'd spent waiting for news of a car crash. . .'

'Mother, it's all right. Please don't upset yourself.'

'Oh, dear! Silly me!' Pamela Carmichael sniffed. 'I haven't thought about it like that for years. I probably *shouldn't* tell you not to marry a doctor. Your temperament would cope with it a lot better than mine.'

'There's no question of my marrying a doctor or anyone else at this stage,' Thea soothed, although marrying a doctor—a particular doctor, Joseph Stockwell—was at this moment the *only* thing she wanted to do.

At his cottage, pacing the newly varnished floors restlessly, Joe was in turmoil as well. Thea had been asking for a commitment from him tonight. In fact, she had been asking him for one for weeks. Spending the night with her this week had set the final seal of certainty on his feelings and he had vowed that he would find that romantic opportunity for a proposal of marriage that he had been yearning for. . .and had been frightened of.

No, it wasn't too soon any more. It was nearly four months since that moonlit night on the Daley's River track, the twelfth of January, when he had first kissed her. His only doubt now was that it was almost too late. She would be leaving Tooma Hospital soon and he didn't know what he was going to ask her to do. There was no work coming up here for a nurse, other than the position that Rosemary Sinclair would be ready to fill again soon.

Things could open up once Sister Drummond retired, but that was still another eighteen months away, and there was no guarantee, even then, of a job for Thea. He had sounded out one of the baby health clinic sisters last week and she had told him that no vacancies were coming up there either. Thea's grandparents were due back in about six weeks. Could Dr Carmichael pull some strings to create a vacancy for her? No, he knew that Thea would not want such a blatant use of family connections.

So what did this mean? Would he suggest a long engagement, with her living in Sydney while he stayed down here? The idea was repugnant to him. Then could he ask her to give up her career in nursing for the sake of being here with him? Could he support them both on his salary when he wanted to spend money improving the cottage and sell it in a few years to move to a bigger place. . .a place with room for children?

He had a sudden horrible vision of himself, Thea

and too many children still crammed into the cottage ten years from now, she dissatisfied with her role as wife and mother because she had been forced to give up her career too soon, he an overworked doctor unwilling to take on an extra partner and lacking the energy to update paintwork and flooring that had once been fresh and attractive, but were now shabby and uncared-for.

A stupid fantasy, he told himself, and unlikely to come true even if Thea did give up her career to marry him. None the less, he knew he could not ask it of her.

Would I move back to Sydney, then, if I had to, so she could go on working? he asked himself. And when the answer came back instantly that of course he would, he knew at last that things were going to be all right.

# CHAPTER TEN

'THERE'S someone to see you, Thea,' Judy Clinton reported at a quarter to two on Thursday afternoon. 'She's waiting out in the foyer. I told her you wouldn't be free for another twenty minutes or so, but I thought I'd better let you know she was here. She said she would wait. I know you've got your mother staying and would like to get back to her as soon as possible, though, so. . .'

'Thanks, Judy,' Thea said, looking up from paperwork at the nurses' station. 'I've got time to see her. But she didn't give her name?'

'No, she didn't. I should have asked. Not someone local—or not someone I recognise, anyway.'

She hurried away along the corridor to check on a patient in early labour, leaving Thea to wonder who her visitor could be, but when she went out to the foyer some minutes later the woman who rose from a rather uncomfortable chair was the last person Thea expected to see.

'Sister Baxter! Hello,' she said carefully, not sure what to expect.

'Not Sister Baxter any more,' the other woman smiled. 'Sister Gledhill. I've gone back to my maiden name. But anyway, please call me Trish.'

Waiting for some dramatic resumption of February's horrible misunderstanding, Thea had been instantly nervous on seeing the director of nursing, but now she knew that the mess had been cleared up. She realised that it could scarcely be otherwise if divorce proceedings were under way and Charmaine and Ewan were openly talking of an engagement.

'Is there somewhere we can go to talk?' the older woman was saying now. 'Do you have time?'

'Yes, I do have time, and there's a café across the street.' Thea saw now that the director of nursing was hesitant about asking for this. 'May I make a phone call first, though?'

She rang her mother quickly, mindful of last Saturday's conversation about Pamela Carmichael waiting anxiously at home anticipating bad news if her loved ones were late. Mrs Carmichael was happy to go on reading her light novel till Thea arrived, saying with a humour that had been missing in her for the past couple of years, 'Stay away until I get past the climax, please!'

A few minutes later, Thea found herself sitting opposite Mount Royal's director of nursing at a small table, waiting for the caramel slice and coffee that each had ordered. Walking her from the hospital she had been able to study Trish Gledhill, as she now called herself, and she saw that there was an inner centre of calm in the woman that had not been there at the beginning of the year. Also, there were deep lines around her eyes and mouth, and some strands of silver in the attractive dark hair now, showing that these months of transition had not been easy ones for Trish.

'It must be obvious to you why I've come,' the director of nursing said, 'and I'm hoping that the fact you've agreed to see me means you'll accept my apology. Apology! That seems inadequate. You lost your job because I wouldn't listen. I. . . I'm leaving Mount Royal but you can be reinstated there as soon as you like.'

'Sister——'

'Trish.'

'Trish, then. You didn't come all this way just to say that, did you?'

'I should have come weeks ago, or phoned, when I first realised that it wasn't you at all who——' Her voice weakened and faltered for a few seconds, then she regained control and said, 'But no, that wasn't the only reason I came down. I've left Mount Royal, as I said, and I'm having a short holiday before moving to Canberra and taking up a position there. My cousin has a place at Narranook, and when I'd tracked you down and realised you were so close I knew it was important that I come to see you. Why didn't you make me listen to the truth three months ago? You've had a terrible time because of it.'

'No, I haven't, actually,' Thea said. 'It has been the best thing that could have happened. I love working at a country hospital, and. . .'

'And you've found love?' the director of nursing came in softly.

'I. . . I think so.'

'You only *think* so?'

'I'm sure of my feelings,' Thea confessed briefly. 'Not of his.'

She didn't know why she was letting herself say these things to a woman she didn't know very well. . . Except that, with all that had happened, she felt she *did* know Trish Gledhill. The director of nursing must have had something of the same sense because they sat over their coffees, refilling them twice, for an hour or more, talking more openly than Thea had talked to another woman for months — about Joe Stockwell, about doubts and certainties, about the nature of love.

Trisha had been badly burned by the failure of her marriage to Ewan Baxter. 'It's ironic,' she said, 'because he was the one who pursued me when I was reluctant. He promised me the moon and stars, undying love, abject slavery almost, if I would marry him, and eventually he won me over. I had terrible doubts about whether I really loved him right up until the wedding-day, then the tables turned. I fell completely in love. . .and he began to lose interest and developed a roving eye. I learned the hard way that extravagant promises don't always add up to what's important.'

'What *does* add up, then?' Thea asked quietly.

Trish laughed. 'I'll let you know if I find out! No, let's think. . . Someone who says less and does more? Someone who *doesn't* tell you it's going to be easy, who *doesn't* promise perfection? Someone who knows what he wants. . .and then waits a while to make absolutely sure? Those are just guesses. Don't look to me for wisdom, Thea! After all, I've failed in that area.'

'You mustn't see it like that,' Thea urged inadequately.

'What, should I blame it all on Ewan and Charmaine?'

'Yes!' They both laughed.

Finally, Thea knew she had to get home for her mother. David was coming down tonight and a special meal had been planned. It was already half-past three and she hoped Mrs Carmichael had been serious about wanting to read that novel. 'I'm very glad you made the effort to see me,' she told the director of nursing.

'So am I,' the older woman said seriously. 'I have a sense of completion now. There's no mess left. I hate mess! Now I can go on to the next stage of my life with no loose ends left from my marriage to Ewan. The divorce, when it comes through, will be just paperwork.'

Impulsively, Thea reached out and touched the older nurse's hand gently, then they both rose to go, agreeing, as they walked back to the hospital, to keep in touch. Trish intended to come down here regularly to use her cousin's beach-house. 'So if you're staying here. . .' she began.

'I'm not,' Thea said, her throat suddenly tight. 'My job here was only temporary. I don't know where I'll be next.'

'And this Joe of yours?'

'He's in partnership down here. He's very happy. I don't think he'd want to move away when he's so recently got established here. I think perhaps that's why he isn't saying anything about our future. He doesn't think there's going to be one.'

Trish Gledhill murmured some sympathetic phrases, but there was nothing, really, that she could say.

Will I manage to pull my life together as bravely as she has done, if it comes to the crunch? Thea wondered. At least she had a good example before her now, proving it could be done.

At the hospital entrance, they said goodbye, since their cars were parked in opposite directions, and Thea hoped that they *would* manage to keep in touch. She might need someone like Trish Gledhill as a guiding light. . .

'Mr King hasn't eaten his lunch again,' Thea reported to Sister Drummond the next afternoon.

'None of it?'

'Not a morsel. He didn't even try. The cutlery is still wrapped in the napkin.'

Joan Drummond snorted and her face set into severe lines. A casual observer might have thought that she was angry with the old man, but Thea knew the director of nursing well enough now to realise that in fact she was heartsore at the idea of their frail old patient giving up his will to live. Ironically, his bronchitis was clearing up well, and he had had no further signs of stroke.

'We could have discharged him on Wednesday if he'd been helping us along,' the director of nursing murmured. 'How long can we justify a hospital bed? Perhaps he should be sent to Dayman Homes up in Wannego. They have an infirmary. I'll discuss it with Dr Stockwell. . .'

There was nothing more to be said for the moment, and they were quite busy. Three new babies slept. . . or wailed. . .in the nursery — Tooma Hospital averaged two or three deliveries a week — and one of them was very jaundiced, needing extra fluids and plenty of exposure to sunlight.

There was another elderly man in for observation this week as well, and he had been placed in Mr King's room in the hope that this would revive the old man's interest in life a little. So far it hadn't worked, and the new patient, Fred Greaves, was demanding and irritable. Sister Drummond had predicted that Dr Fane would send him to Wollongong tomorrow for tests.

Thea spent the next hour back and forth between her different charges, moving the sun-lamp from yellow-tinted baby Thompson to baby Thompson's mother, who needed the soothing warmth to help heal her episiotomy. Sister Drummond was caught up on the phone, and then came word that another woman was on her way in with labour pains. 'That'll be five babies this week, and next week we'll probably have none,' the director of nursing said. 'Which just goes to show that averages don't help much in predicting your workload.'

She laughed comfortably, and Thea joined in. Her shift would be over in less than an hour and she was having to make an effort to concentrate now. Last Saturday she had promised to spend the evening. . . and the night. . .at Joe's and they had agreed then that in the meantime it would be difficult, and probably impossible, to meet and talk. That had proved an accurate prediction, and now Thea was feeling out of touch.

A snatched word with him here and there in the corridors of the hospital, some brief, very medical exchanges over the phone or over a patient, called in very early this morning to help him deliver the third of the nursery's current crop of babies. . .and talking to Trish yesterday, voicing her doubts, had confirmed the fact that in spite of all their times of closeness she didn't know where she stood in his life. There was a stark truth that she knew she had to face: sometimes love, no matter how promising it seemed at the start, did not work out.

David and Mrs Carmichael had left after breakfast this morning. Thea had been able to take a short break from the hospital, after the newest baby's safe arrival, in order to say goodbye to them, but when Mrs Carmichael had asked when they would next see each other she hadn't known what to say.

'You finish here in two weeks, don't you?' Pamela Carmichael had said.

'Two and a half,' Thea corrected her quickly, wanting to stretch the time out in her mind to be as long as it could.

'I suppose you'll come back to us and start looking for another job.'

'I should think so,' Thea found herself saying. 'As it turns out, I could go back to Mount Royal if I wanted to, but I'd rather have a change. I think perhaps a smaller hospital in the outlying suburbs. . .'

'No need to rush into anything,' Mrs Carmichael said with unusual gentleness. 'Better to wait a while and make the right decision.'

'I know. . .'

David had rattled the car keys impatiently at that

point, embarrassed about the emotion he sensed underlying mother's and daughter's words, and Thea knew that she had to get back to work, too. Her break had already been generous and Barbara Dawes was waiting to go home. Climbing into her grandmother's car, she had followed David and Mrs Carmichael along the road from Conway Bay to Tooma, then the latter two had turned on to the highway and sped up out of sight, while she had found her usual side-street parking place.

Now, at ten to two, she would soon be back at the car and on her way home, with three hours to fill in before the time she had agreed to be at Joe's. . .

'Sister Carmichael?' the director of nursing had entered the nursery quietly, waiting until Thea had finished the last of three nappy changes before speaking.

'Yes, Sister. Sorry, was I —— ?'

'It's Mr King,' Joan Drummond said. 'He has died, I'm afraid, some time in the last half-hour. Mr Greaves has been in the patients' sitting-room so we can't know exactly how or when it happened.'

'Oh, no!'

'Well,' the older woman sighed, 'we've all been expecting it, in our heart of hearts, haven't we?'

'Yes, but. . . I wondered if he would rally.'

'I didn't think so,' the director of nursing admitted, out of her long experience. 'He's been steadily going down since his daughter left on Monday. I thought the end would come peacefully in his sleep, and it seems to have done just that. No one heard him move or cry out. I've phoned Dr Stockwell to come in. He should be here very soon. Would you phone Mr King's son and daughter? I have to get back to the front office. Something else has come up there.'

'Should I take the babies to their mothers first? It's just about two o'clock feed time.'

'Yes, go ahead. A few minutes' delay in ringing won't matter. We may not be able to get the son in the middle of the day anyway. I think we only have his home number. Check the patient record card.'

'Mmm-hmm,' Thea nodded.

One at a time, she ferried the three tiny babies across the corridor from the bright nursery to the mothers in their rooms, feeling as she had never felt in large Mount Royal's busy atmosphere the truth that death and life were inextricably blended together. These little morsels of life, so miraculously warm and tender and perfect, had just begun their journeys, while just a short distance along the corridor someone else's journey had ended. Somehow, it took away the sadness a little.

Ten minutes later, she had talked to Joanne Aitkens, who had said that she would phone her brother Paul with the news. Then Thea went along to Mr King's room, where Joe had made his official pronouncement that life was extinguished. Mr King would now be moved away to the hospital's small morgue until arrangements were made for his funeral.

Judy Clinton had arrived now and Thea was off duty but she wanted to say some sort of goodbye to the patient who had been in and out of her life since she had first come to Tooma almost three months ago. Standing in the doorway, she watched Joe for a moment. He had just finished his brief examination and was ready to leave the room, while behind him Mr King's eyes were peacefully closed.

'Hi,' Joe said softly to her and they both turned away. 'Going home now?'

'Yes,' she nodded, her jaw trembling suddenly as she said the brief syllable. He saw it.

'Don't,' he said. 'Come into the office for a minute and sit down. Should I get you some tea?'

'No, don't be silly. I'm fine. But would *you* like some?'

'Can't stay long. Just have to do the paperwork.'

'I should go, then.'

'No!' His grasp of her hand was authoritative and seconds later she was in the small office across the corridor with him alone, and the door had shut behind them.

Without words, he took her in his arms and held her closely against him, his touch, his warmth and his weight taking away the sadness left by Mr King's death as well as her sense of bereavement at not seeing Joe — not like this — for a whole week. For the moment, she didn't care that the future was still unresolved between them, she just needed these moments and needed to live in them completely.

When his mouth came down to close over hers, drinking her kiss thirstily, she let her own mouth taste him fully and lifted her hands to run them through his hair so that afterwards she could catch the faint almond scent of his shampoo on her fingers.

'Oh, Joe. . .' she breathed against his mouth and he began to kiss her even more urgently. . .until there was a sudden click as the office door opened and Sister Drummond stood there, witnessing everything before the shocked couple could rouse themselves enough to pull apart.

The director of nursing wore a glacial expression and her stance was warlike. Thea had never seen her like this before, though she had known all along that the role of dragon would be an accomplished one in Joan Drummond's repertoire.

'I hope you are going to tell me that my eyes were deceiving me,' she rumbled ominously, her heavy bosom jutting forward like weaponry. 'Since you're both well aware that this hospital frowns on intimate relationships between staff, and why that is so.'

Joe stepped forward, his gaze and voice steady. 'Sister Drummond, it won't happen again, I assure you. And I can also assure you that it won't bring any undesirable scandal to the hospital. Sister Carmichael and I are — er — engaged. He stopped and cleared his throat. 'That's surely not in violation of hospital policy?'

'Engaged?' Her eyes narrowed suspiciously. 'That's odd.' She clamped shut her mouth, clearly at a loss for the moment.

All three of them were silent, while Thea thought, He *had* to say that. It doesn't mean he really wanted to. I'll have to make it clear to him that he doesn't have to honour a commitment made out of desperation like that.

The director of nursing had recovered her equilibrium somewhat by this time. 'Does this mean. . .' she narrowed her eyes even further '. . . that you might be interested in continuing on at the hospital, Sister Carmichael? Or do you have plans for other employment once your contract with us is ended?'

'I. . . I have no other plans, but — '

Rosemary Sinclair has just informed me this afternoon that she *won't* be returning from her maternity leave after all. The two days she worked her while you were with your mother in Sydney convinced her that she wasn't ready to come back to work. In fact, she has resigned. So there is now the opportunity for you to stay on.'

'I'll have to think about it,' Thea answered slowly.

She saw Joe's startled, wary glance but couldn't do anything about it. She had embarrassed both of them three and a half weeks ago, suggesting that they consider themselves engaged. She *wasn't* going to back him into a corner about it now!

'Hmm. . .' The director of nursing was clearly not pleased. Was she angered at Thea's hesitation, or suspicious that perhaps no genuine engagement existed? Again, there was a silence and Thea found that she was holding her breath. The sister said, 'Well, please make your decision soon. Today is the twelfth. The hospital needs to know by the seventeenth, and that is all that matters to me. And now. . .aren't you finished here for the day, Sister Carmichael?'

'Yes, I am. I was just going,' Thea murmured quickly. The date that the director of nursing had mentioned kept drumming in her mind and she realised that it was exactly four months ago today when she and Joe had kissed for the first time, under the moonlight that shone on Mount Aspiring. Not a good time to be thinking about such whimsical, romantic things. . .

Joan Drummond stood aside for her to pass through the door and on down the corridor and there was nothing to be done but leave the building and go home. It seemed a long time until six o'clock when she had said that she would go to Joe's.

Sensing that, after what had happened this afternoon and after the time they hadn't seen each other over her mother's visit, something would have to be resolved between them tonight, Thea dressed up a little, choosing a cocktail-length dress of pale green jersey and adding a gold chain necklace and matching bracelet. If Joe wanted to tell her that there was no real engagement between them, that he didn't think they had a future together any more, she could at least gain some courage and backbone from being prettily dressed!

*Would* he say those things? She really didn't know. There were times when she felt so certain that her love for him was fully matched and returned, but at other times things got in the way. She had been foolish to be jealous over Jessica Lewis, far too tense about the secrecy they had to keep up. . . Had these things taken the glow off his feelings?

When she arrived at his cottage that night, the autumn dusk had begun to close in already and the lights were on inside, making a soft yellow glow through the windows. He met her at the door before she even knocked, pulling her in and spinning her round to admire the dress that clung to her slender curves on top and flared from a gathered waist below.

The sitting-room looked homey now, not yet fully renovated but with attractive sheets thrown over the awful old couch, the worst of the wallpaper stripped and tonight a crackling little fire in the grate as the evening was quite chilly.

'You dressed up,' Joe said.

'So did you.' He was wearing dark tailored trousers and a raw silk shirt in a green that almost matched her dress.

'I thought we might go out later,' he said.

'Go out?'

'Yes. In public. To a restaurant. Don't you think it's time there were no more secrets, Thea?' he whispered, engulfing her in his arms and saying the words with an intensity that made them rasp in his throat.

'No more secrets? That would be wonderful!' Her own voice trembled a little.

'We've nearly been destroyed by them. . . We really aren't very good at subterfuge, are we?' he said, pulling away.

'No!' she readily agreed, wishing he had stayed close to her. He had moved right away now, as if preparing to say something important. . .and hurtful? Surely not!

'Today was a mess, wasn't it?' he said now.

'You mean. . .in the office? Sister Drummond?'

'Yes. Do you think she believed my story of an engagement?'

'I don't know. She did at first, I think, but then. . .'

'I guess it just wasn't very convincing,' he went on, sighing in an exaggerated way. 'We didn't quite *look* engaged, did we? We didn't quite feel it.'

'No, I suppose not,' she managed to return in a small voice.

Then suddenly he was beside her again, holding a small black velvet box. 'Do you think this would make the picture more convincing?' he whispered.

And there was a ring—a slim gold band set with a row of five small diamonds that sparkled as the ring caught the light. He pulled it from its velvet nest and slipped it on to the third finger of her left hand. 'Look! It even fits!'

'It's. . .beautiful,' Thea said throatily.

'It was just a guess. A ring is a very personal thing. Go to the jeweller's and choose another one, or at least look. . .'

'Silly! You *do* know my taste! I love this; it's simple and pretty and. . .'

'And does it mean now, that we're really engaged?'

'Yes. . .'

'Thank goodness for that! I've wanted to ask you to marry me for a long time, Thea.'

'Then why didn't you?' she whispered, gazing up at him.

He told her—how at first it had seemed too soon, then too much the influence of circumstances they both disliked. How he had been waiting for the perfect moment. . . 'And then it seemed as if I would be asking you to give up your career.'

'I would have done.'

'But reluctantly.'

'Yes.'

'I finally realised last week that if I didn't want you
to slip through my fingers. . .' he slipped her silky dark
blonde hair through those fingers as he spoke '. . . I
had to stop hanging back, start trusting that we could
get through those obstacles together. I realised I'd give
up the partnership here and go back to Sydney if that
was what you wanted. *Is* it what you want? You seemed
hesitant about the job here today?'

'Only because I'd begun to doubt that you saw a
future for us together.'

'*Never* doubt that, my dear darling!' He gave convincing proof of his sincerity with his passionate mouth.

After this, there was not much of importance left to
say. He had bought champagne and they sprawled by
the fire together, sipping it lazily and talking the sort
of nonsense that lovers had always talked and that
Thea decided was the most delicious nonsense in the
world. Joe had remembered the significance of today's
date as well, which led to all sorts of delicious rediscov-
eries. Then they went to dinner, holding hands as they
walked down the front steps, driving in the same car,
stopping to kiss briefly at the door of the restaurant,
right in front of a member of the hospital board.

And when Eileen McCredie came up to them at their
table to say, 'It's our bowling club dinner tonight, and
all the ladies over there want to know what you're
doing here, Dr Stockwell. Is it a special celebration?'
Joe answered in a voice that could be heard by at least
four other tables,

'A celebration? It certainly is! It's our anniversary.
We've been together for four months now.'

'Four months? But. . . I thought that you and Jessica
Lewis —— ?'

'Appearances can be deceptive, Mrs McCredie.'

'I'll say! And some people are very good at keeping
secrets!'

'I'm not keeping this a secret,' Thea came in, holding out her left hand, where a diamond ring sparkled in the candlelight. Under the table, her right hand was happily imprisoned in Joe's warm, firm clasp.

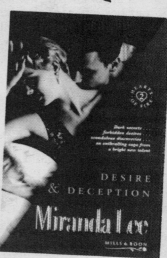
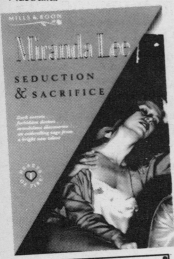

# LOVE ON CALL
# 4 FREE BOOKS AND 2 FREE GIFTS
## FROM MILLS & BOON

Capture all the drama and emotion of a hectic medical world when you accept 4 Love on Call romances PLUS a cuddly teddy bear and a mystery gift - absolutely FREE and without obligation. And, if you choose, go on to enjoy 4 exciting Love on Call romances every month for only £1.80 each! Be sure to return the coupon below today to: Mills & Boon Reader Service, FREEPOST, PO Box 236, Croydon, Surrey CR9 9EL.

--- **NO STAMP REQUIRED** ---

**YES!** Please rush me 4 FREE Love on Call books and 2 FREE gifts! Please also reserve me a Reader Service subscription, which means I can look forward to receiving 4 brand new Love on Call books for only £7.20 every month, postage and packing FREE. If I choose not to subscribe, I shall write to you within 10 days and still keep my FREE books and gifts. I may cancel or suspend my subscription at any time. I am over 18 years. Please write in BLOCK CAPITALS.

Ms/Mrs/Miss/Mr _____  **EP63D**

Address _____

_____

Postcode _____ Signature _____

mps
MAILING
PREFERENCE
SERVICE

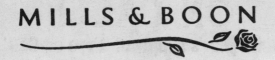

# MILLS & BOON

# LOVE ON CALL

## The books for enjoyment this month are:

**NO MORE SECRETS** Lilian Darcy
**TILL SUMMER ENDS** Hazel Fisher
**TAKE A DEEP BREATH** Margaret O'Neill
**HEALING LOVE** Meredith Webber

♥   ♥   ♥   ♥   ♥

## Treats in store!

Watch next month for the following absorbing stories:

**VET IN A QUANDARY** Mary Bowring
**NO SHADOW OF DOUBT** Abigail Gordon
**PRIORITY CARE** Mary Hawkins
**TO LOVE AGAIN** Laura MacDonald

# ON CALL!

## Win a year's supply of 'Love on Call' romances ABSOLUTELY FREE?

**Yes**, you can win one whole year's supply of 'Love on Call' romances! It's easy! All you have to do is convert the four sets of numbers below into television soaps by using the letters in the telephone dial. Fill in your answers plus your name and address details overleaf, cut out and send to us by 30th Sept. 1994.

1  5233315767 _____

2  3552 152 1819 _____

3  165547322 _____

4  2177252267 _____

**Please turn over for entry details**

# ON CALL!

## SEND YOUR ENTRY NOW!

The first five correct entries picked out of the bag after the closing date will each win one year's supply of 'Love on Call' romances (four books every month - worth over £85). What could be easier?

Don't forget to enter your name and address in the space below then put this page in an envelope and post it today (you don't need a stamp). Competition closes 30th Sept. '94.

**'Love on Call' Competition
FREEPOST
P.O. Box 236
Croydon
Surrey CR9 9EL**

- - - - - - - - - - - - - - - - - - - - - - - - - - - - - - - - - - - - - - - - - ✈

EPLQ

Are you a Reader Service subscriber?     Yes ☐          No ☐

Ms/Mrs/Miss/Mr _____

Address _____

_____

_____

_____ Postcode _____

Signature _____